ME
DEC

BY
LISA COOPER

MILLS & BOON LIMITED
ETON HOUSE 18–24 PARADISE ROAD
RICHMOND SURREY TW9 1SR

First published in Great Britain 1991
by Mills & Boon Limited

© Lisa Cooper 1991

Australian copyright 1991
Philippine copyright 1991
This edition 1991

ISBN 0 263 77453 8

Set in 10½ on 12 pt Linotron Times
03-9111-52116
Typeset in Great Britain by Centracet, Cambridge
Made and printed in Great Britain

CHAPTER ONE

'HE's just a great big boy who had lots of sisters to run around after him,' Staff Nurse Dahlia Stephens said in a soothing voice. Nurse Patricia Metcalf smiled and wondered just what the doctor was really like, as she saw the back of his unbuttoned white coat flapping away down the corridor as if the man had a train to catch.

Sister Stafford gave a very unladylike snort. 'Well, he can get used to putting his gown and gloves in the bin and leaving the sink tidy after he cleans up,' she replied. She noticed the junior nurse standing by the door, hesitating but obviously wanting to speak to her. 'What is it, Nurse?' she asked crossly, her annoyance with the guilty doctor spilling over into her tone of voice.

'I'm Nurse Metcalf, and I was told to report to Men's Surgical, Sister. I'm one of the set just out of Block,' Tricia added, as she had the impression that Sister Stafford had no idea who she was and didn't expect to see her on her ward.

'Ah, yes. Well, Nurse, you'd better help Staff Nurse.'

'We're all up straight until dressings, Sister. Shall I give Nurse Metcalf a report?' Dahlia's brown eyes twinkled. 'I can give report to both of the new nurses,' she said. 'We had a memo that we can expect two from the last batch with Sister Tutor, and the new Block can't begin until the roof of the annexe and lecture-rooms has been repaired after the storm damage, so the nurses due there to replace them have to stay with us for a while, and that means we have a lot of staff.'

'I know. That means we have two extra nurses until further notice. Why is it that when we're rushed off our feet we have to make do with very few staff and when we're slack, as we are now, we're deluged with new nurses?'

Sister didn't wait for a reply but went to answer the low buzz emanating from the internal telephone. 'Action?' she murmured hopefully. 'Sister Stafford, Ward Seven.'

She listened carefully and held up a hand to stop the two nurses leaving the office, nodded once or twice and put down the receiver.

'An emergency?' asked Dahlia.

'Anything but that, unless you count an epidemic of gastro-enteritis at St Thomas's our business. Here we are with too many nurses, while they have to close wards for a while until the infection has gone, and the nurses have gone back on duty.'

'Do they want some of us to help? I didn't know we were in their sector.'

'Not that, but they want us to take over their Alexandra Rose Day collection in the Strand. Usually our nurses go to Dulwich and Camberwell, but as Sister Tutor has had to cancel the next Block for tuition in the annexe, since the storm blew away half the roof, we can spare someone to help.' Sister looked at the memo on the desk. 'Nurse Allen is coming from Block too.' She glanced at the neatly uniformed girl in front of her and approved the dark, gently curling hair that framed an attractive, piquant face, the spotless uniform and the well polished shoes.

Nurse Patricia Metcalf looked apprehensive. It was bad enough coming to a men's ward for the first time after only a few months of training, and a further month of tutoring that had, for her, broken the routine of ward work and made all her early fears return, but now Sister was looking at her as if she had something even more terrifying in store for her, and as usual when she was scared her deep blue eyes widened to make her look startled.

'It's all right, Nurse,' Dahlia reassured her in a warm voice that the patients found comforting, just as they liked her strong firm brown arms and her gentle touch. 'I did it once and enjoyed meeting all those people who wanted to know where I worked and where I was from, and I even had a few men trying to date me.' Her shoulders shook with suppressed laughter as Tricia looked even more disturbed.

'Yes, you and Nurse Allen, wherever she might be, will report to the front entrance near Casualty in ten minutes with the other nurses who are going, and be taken by mini-bus to the West End. There you'll be given collecting boxes and trays of Rose Day stickers. At four this afternoon you will be collected again and brought back here, where a hospital charity organiser will take the boxes and the remaining roses.'

'Do we take anything else, Sister? I thought we were never allowed out of the hospital grounds in uniform.'

'Today is the one exception, and you must take your cloak. It's a warm day for spring, but it could get chilly waiting on street corners. When you return you must put the uniform you wear into the laundry and wear fresh tomorrow on the wards.'

'They'll be there a long time, Sister. When do they get something to eat?' Dahlia pointed out gently.

'I suppose they'll have to have a break,' Sister admitted reluctantly. 'When a nurse has to accompany a patient by ambulance to a unit many miles away, she has an allowance for food, so I suppose this comes into that category.' She opened a petty cash box in the office drawer and handed out enough money for two lunches and emergency bus fares. 'For both of you,' she said. 'You might not need to take a bus as you're to be fetched at four, but you never know,' she added darkly. 'So save enough for fares, unless you take some money of your own with you.'

'Sister? I'm Nurse Allen, reporting.' The pretty blonde girl who had been listening smiled at Tricia as much as to say, nice to be working together, then looked deceptively solemn as Sister Stafford glanced at the wall clock and frowned.

'You're late, Nurse. Now hurry up, and Nurse

Metcalf will tell you what's happening. Another five minutes and you would have missed the bus!'

'Missed the bus? Waiting on street corners? What gives, Tricia? I never thought I'd hear a senior nursing officer tell me to go and hang about on street corners. What *would* my dear old granny say?' laughed Nurse Allen.

'You heard most of what she said, so you know where we're going. Have you any money with you? Sister gave me lunch money, but we might want to spend more. Tell the driver to wait for me and I'll get some from the hostel.' Tricia ran off across the drive, leaving her friend giggling and still unsure of what they had to do.

Six other nurses had already climbed into the mini-bus, all looking smart and fresh, with the same message ringing in their ears from various seniors. 'Remember, Nurse, that you're a representative of the Princess Beatrice Hospital and so must at all times when in uniform behave with dignity and courtesy.'

'What if we sell all our roses and have time to spare? Can we take in a matinee?' asked Josephine Allen when Tricia sank breathlessly into her seat.

'Of course not!' Tricia replied in a shocked voice. 'We're on duty in a way, and I have a feeling we shall stand about and try to look interested while the whole of London flows past us and doesn't notice what we're doing. I hate the idea.'

'No, a theatre isn't poss,' Josie agreed. 'They might think we were selling ice-creams if we went in with a tray in the dark!' She sat back and watched the first wave of people hurrying to work. 'I thought it was only nurses who had to get up at some ungodly hour to go on duty, but there seem to be a few more out here. They all look far too hassled to pause to buy a paper rose or a sticker, but we might catch the executives who get to their offices later.'

'You were late on duty,' said Tricia. 'I saw you at breakfast and you seemed ready. What kept you?'

'I came through Casualty and saw the most heavenly man talking to Sister King, so I hung about for five minutes in case he needed first aid!'

'You are a nut!' laughed Tricia. What really happened?'

'Partly true. Sister nabbed me to take some notes up to a ward on my way on duty. She seemed to want him all to herself, which isn't what we've been taught. Never get involved with a patient, they say, but she wanted to *eat* him!'

'Maybe he wasn't a patient. He might have been one of the staff, or her boyfriend making an early call,' Tricia replied mildly.

'Maybe.' Josie frowned. 'There was a crumpled white coat lying on a trolley as if he might have thrown it there, but he was wearing a tracksuit. Not really my type, but very, very macho, with good shoulders and rather nice thick bronzy hair.' She laughed. 'Not your type either, ducky. Far too untidy for nice tidy little Nurse Metcalf. I bet you brought a clean hanky and a few pieces of tissue in case the public loos have run out!'

'And who'll want to have some if she needs it?' Tricia asked drily, but her mind was on the glint of reddish-brown hair worn thick and needing a cut, and the waft of clean masculinity that had been left when the doctor had hurried from the clinical-room, carelessly leaving everything untidy as if he had far more important matters on his mind. Men with that colour hair often had green eyes or hazel with touches of grey, she thought, then touched her cap to make sure it sat straight and wondered why she was so sure that the man in Casualty was the same one. I didn't even see him properly, she decided. He may have spots and a cruel mouth—but somehow she wasn't convinced.

'Next stop Westminster Bridge,' the hospital driver called. 'Pick you up at ten past four over there, Nurses.'

Two nurses got down and a woman with a car boot full of collecting trays handed out boxes and trays to them and to the other nurses who remained in the bus. 'Don't show any hospital badges,' she advised. 'When I was in training we did wear them and the public liked to know, but now it's different.' She sighed. 'Be careful, girls. Never say where you live if men try to chat you up, as there have been times when nurses have been harassed if they gave the name of their hospital.'

The bus drove on to the Strand and left Tricia and Josie on the corner of Trafalgar Square. 'What does she think we are?' asked Josie. 'We aren't likely to get picked up in this gear! Unless it's by men with a fetish for girls in black tights and nurse's uniform.'

'Shut up and smile,' Tricia advised her. She held out her box, and within a few minutes a small line of office workers had given generously and taken stickers. Middle-aged men expected her to put the rose on their lapels or anoraks and seemed pleased to have a pretty girl smiling at them, while a group of schoolchildren on the way to a cultural trip in an art gallery looked envious, as if they wished they could be nurses and do such interesting work! 'I wonder if they'd look like that if they saw the sluice in Ward Six,' Tricia said. 'I hope men aren't too difficult as patients. I was scared this morning when I saw all those faces staring at me as I went through the ward. Gynae and Kids' were great, but I hate the thought of nursing men.'

'Let me guess. All-female boarding school and no brothers? Stayed on for further education as head girl until you were old enough to get into Beattie's?'

'Josephine Allen, you're psychic!' Tricia admitted with a touch of resentment. 'Is it so obvious? I've never really belonged to one place for long enough to settle and get to know people, so my old school was really home to me whenever my parents were abroad. Dad's in the Navy, and they've been based in all kinds of places where I couldn't go to school for long enough to get any qualifications.'

'Nice holidays, though?'

'Great! Oman was wonderful. I saw the turtles laying eggs on a beach there in an area where only Brits working there are allowed, but no tourists.'

'I've seen pictures,' said Josie. 'The men look dreamy. Did you ever fall under the spell of dark brown eyes and fierce hawklike features?'

'Do you ever think of anything but men?' laughed

Tricia. 'But no, I didn't. I learned to scuba-dive there, and it was far too hot for anything in places where there was no air-conditioning.' She laughed. 'We even had to swim wearing T-shirts as the sun was so strong we could get burned through the water. I wonder how they manage to have so many children in such places? Hot nights must be one big turn-off.'

'We represent all the hospitals,' Josie said evasively, when a man bent a little too close and tried to take her hand when she offered him a rose. 'No, we're not with one unit,' she lied. 'In fact we're just moving again, and haven't really been told where we shall be next week,' which Tricia decided was almost the truth, and she nodded in agreement.

'Go about in pairs, I see,' the main persisted, and stood with coins ready to put in the box, but he stayed close as if he had the right to chat up the attractive nurses.

'Well, put the money in the box if you want a rose,' Josie told him. 'Others are waiting.'

Reluctantly, he dropped several coins in the box and took a rose, stepping back to allow two women to buy stickers. Twice he tried to make conversation, until a policeman strolled by as if by accident and asked how they were doing. 'Fine,' Tricia said, and gave him a very relieved smile.

'You'll get a bit of that from his sort,' he said comfortably. 'But I think you can handle it, and I'll be around from time to time. I had a bell from the organisers. If you go for lunch, leave the money in the bank over there and they'll give you empty boxes so that you have no money with you where you go to eat. They'll label your box so that they know which hospital sent you and see that you get the right tally tonight. We haven't lost a box yet in this area, but you never know.'

'Thanks,' said Tricia. 'It's nice to feel protected.'

'A pleasure,' he replied, and Josie raised her eyebrows when at last he was called on his radio and left reluctantly, after lingering even more than the man he had frightened off.

'A slight improvement, but not a lot,' was her opinion. 'I think I need a change of scene. Let's go along there.'

'We were told to stay in this area, Josie. There are other nurses and voluntary workers covering other places. Anyway, it's nearly time to eat, if twelve isn't too early. I'm starving, and we ought to be back to catch the lunch crowds. I heard that Lyons Corner House have a place along there, so we can leave our money in the bank on the way.'

'We didn't stop for elevenses,' Josie recalled. 'We've earned our grub. I haven't seen the restaurant since it's been re-done as it was in the twenties or thirties or whenever it was when the girls wore those frilly caps and aprons like Victorian parlourmaids. A bit like the old Beattie's caps and quite sexy.'

They handed in the now heavy boxes and received the empty ones, suddenly aware that they might be carrying quite a lot of money.

The spiral staircase cut the restaurant into bright

levels with fresh green and white décor and attractive tables and chairs, and they ordered lasagne and coffee and enjoyed sitting down after standing on hard pavements all morning. It was very comfortable, and half guiltily they ordered more coffee and two huge pavlovas.

'This is far more immoral than sex in the afternoon,' Josie said cheerfully. 'Not that I've tried,' she added when she saw Tricia's horrified expression. 'Wishful thinking, and after seeing a sample of London life today, I can't say it appeals much outside a good romantic novel. You must have met hundreds of nice clean and randy sailors. Have you anything to tell Auntie Josephine, my dear?'

'Not really,' said Tricia. 'I do meet quite a lot, but as my father is usually their commander they take it easy and stand off a bit, and I've learned that the ones I like are mostly married or so footloose that I steer clear of trouble. They're fun for an evening, but I don't date them unless we're in a group.' She laughed a bit uneasily. 'They shift around the world and are a rootless lot until they marry and have enough rank to take a wife with them, so now I avoid the lonely bachelors who really do have a girl in every port.'

'You said *now* you avoid them?'

Tricia blushed. 'It did happen once. I believed every word he said, then luckily I found out he was having it off with at least three girls in the UK, South Africa and Oman. He wanted to have a picture of me and took some snaps, but a friend of his was passing just as the shutter clicked and he called out, "One more for the harem, Mike?" I saw from his face that it wasn't a joke, so I did *not* go away with him for the weekend as we'd planned, but made a few enquiries and was sick to my stomach, as the Yanks say.'

'He sounds fine to me,' Josie said. 'I think it's a mistake to get tied up to any one man too soon.'

'It's put me off men,' Tricia said shortly.

'I suppose it's as well to be cautious, with this Aids scare, but if you're too careful you'll end up a saintly virgin with a tabby cat,' Josie warned her. 'Give a little and lie back and enjoy it. My current boyfriend has a mate, and we could have a foursome one evening, when we have a day off to follow and can be out late.'

'I'll let you know,' Tricia said laconically, thinking that Josie's men were a bit on the physical side from what she had seen when they came to fetch her from the hostel, and she hated men who breathed beer over her. Some men smelled good at all times. She noticed a smartly dressed man threading his way between the now crowded tables, who as he passed left a scent of good aftershave and soap. She took a deep breath and was almost in the clinical-room again with the back view of a man hurrying from the room and leaving just such an ambience. She gave a wry smile. The figure almost flying down the corridor had been no male model with immaculate clothes, and yet she sensed that he was. . .what? Different? Or just clean?

'Back to the streets,' Josie said. 'I shall write and

tell my mother what I did today and how many times I was accosted.'

London seemed much busier now, and several times the nurses had to step back to avoid being pushed around by hurrying figures who ignored them, and the sky darkened, making them glad they wore thick cloaks. The young policeman came back, but was too busy to linger, and another man tried to date Josie, who told him at last that she was on duty until nine but would meet him at the entrance to the British Museum at half past nine. 'That should settle his hash!' she muttered as he went away smirking with triumph. 'How many is it that will line up to meet us outside the Museum tonight? I make it about eight!' Two women with bulging shopping bags pushed past them, sending Josie flying into the gutter.

'It's only half past two and we've no hope of being collected until four,' grumbled Tricia. 'Are you all right?' She took one look at Josie's pale face and made her sit on the low wall by a shop.

'It's my stupid ankle—I slipped over the kerb. Damn! I had enough physio for a whole rugby team last year for that, but I've played tennis since then. I thought it would be fine for ever, but now it's done it again, or is it the other one? I forget. All I know is that it's agony!' sighed Josie.

'You'd better get back to Beattie's and report to Cas. I've got some money and you can get a taxi, but I'd better stay here for the mini-bus or they'll think I've been abducted! Can you manage at the other end?' asked Tricia.

'I've enough money and I can yell for help if I see a nice male student with big strong arms,' said Josie. She sat still until the taxi drew up as close as it could and the driver helped her into the back seat. Tricia stood by the road and waved, worried that Josie might not be able to walk from the taxi to Casualty, then she let her arm fall to her side as she recalled that many casualties arrived at the entrance by cab or private car and staff were ready with wheelchairs if necessary.

She backed away from the dusty car that had stopped by the pavement on double yellow lines.

'Get in and I'll take you back to the hospital,' a deep voice said.

'No, there's no need, thank you. I didn't wave for a taxi. I waved to a friend,' she said weakly.

'I'm not a taxi!' The voice was growing angry. 'For Pete's sake get in and save me from that frosty-looking meter maid rapidly approaching.'

'I have to stay here to be collected,' Tricia insisted, backing away as he opened the car door.

'I've been asked to pick you up,' the man said. 'Come on, Nurse, I'm not going to bite you!'

'I have no idea who you are, and I don't accept lifts from strangers,' said Tricia, then felt like a child repeating the safety lesson learned in school.

'Get in,' he repeated harshly, but she shook her head. 'Oh, please yourself, I'm not going to drag you into the car, but you won't find another lift today. Your mini-bus has been cancelled and I haven't time to waste on little fools. There are other nurses on the other side of the Square waiting, so

I'll pick them up first and come back for you if by then you've decided I'm not Jack the Ripper and you remember that you do know me, or at least must have seen me at the hospital. When that traffic warden asks questions, just say I wanted to know the way to Oxford Circus!'

'Who are you?' Tricia asked the empty air as he drove away. Her hands trembled as she clutched the tray of stickers.

'Everything all right, love?' It was the friendly policeman again.

'I'm not sure.' She hesitated. The man in the car had not threatened her and had given no sign of violence, but his voice and manner had been compelling as if he was used to having his own way.

'Tried to pick you up, did he?' She saw that the policeman was serious.

'He offered me a lift back to the hospital,' she told him, not wanting to make a meal of the situation.

'Right! Now take my advice, miss, and get a taxi back to Beattie's. About lunchtime, two nurses were accosted within five minutes of each other and one was badly frightened by a man in a car trying to pick her up. The girls aren't from your lot, but the organisers alerted all hospitals who sent out nurses today, and volunteers are rounding up collectors and sending them home early in case he gets really nasty.' The policeman grinned. 'Can't really blame him—the sight of all that crisp uniform is enough to turn on men a lot more sane than he must be. Where's your friend?'

'She twisted her ankle and went back by taxi, but I thought I must wait for the mini-bus,' Tricia told him.

'Not nice to be here alone. I'll get you a taxi. You can catch a bus over there, but there's a very long wait and I want you safely away from the Strand and Trafalgar Square.' The policeman took out his note-book. 'Just give me an idea what this character looks like. Make of car?' She shook her head and he sighed. 'Right. Description?'

'I think he wore a tracksuit of dark blue—no, green. His hair was darkish with red in it and his eyes were. . .angry.' She frowned. Were they grey or green? It was difficult to say, but she remembered them as she recalled vividly the firm mouth that hinted at other moods beyond the immediate irri-tation, the full sensual lower lip and the slight cleft in the rugged chin. 'I don't think he meant any harm,' she added.

'Never think that. Better to be safe than sorry, Nurse, and take my word for it, there are men who look as innocent as a bishop and can do some very nasty things.'

The policeman raised a hand and from the muddle of traffic a cab slid to a halt beside them. 'Nicked you, did he, Nurse?' the driver said with a grin. 'Where to, Officer? Southwark or the Tower of London?'

'The Princess Beatrice Hospital, mate, and don't lose her. Keep an eye open for a dusty car driven by a man with ginger hair and wearing a tracksuit. He's got a thing about nurses.'

'No wonder. Shouldn't be allowed out looking like that,' the driver said with feeling. 'Hop in, Nurse, and keep your eyes peeled. If you spot him I'll radio in.'

'Not ginger hair!' Tricia murmured. How could anyone call glossy brown hair with red highlights, that looked squeaky clean and soft, ginger? 'What about the mini-bus?' she asked as the door opened. 'Has it really been cancelled?'

'It wasn't available so early and members of staff at the various hospitals have offered to bring their own nurses home.'

The policeman slammed the door and waved the cab on. Tricia sat back and crumpled two stickers into a tight ball. He'd said the mini-bus wouldn't be coming as if he really knew. A tight feeling in her midriff made her wonder if she wanted to be sick as she recalled his last words to her. He did come from Beattie's! He had arrogantly supposed she must know him or know of him, and his voice was a voice that hinted at culture, confidence and power. He hadn't touched her, and yet it seemed he had made a kind of contact that left her half afraid and half attracted.

Don't be ridiculous, she told herself. The policeman was right, she decided firmly. A man on the make, or a man after a girl, could make his victim believe anything. He was just a cheap kerb-crawler.

Casualty seemed like a familiar friend as Tricia paid off the cab driver, who refused a tip, saying he might need her one day. 'Take care, now,' he called,

and she smiled at the Americanism that sat awkwardly on Cockney lips.

Somehow she must get rid of the charity tray, and
Casualty seemed the best place to ask about it, and
besides, Josie might be there if her ankle had needed
treatment. Other trays were on a table and a charity
organiser was emptying boxes and counting the
money. 'Oh, good. Just two more to come in with
Dr Clancy. Is he coming in here? I want to thank
him for helping out.' The woman glanced towards
the open door. 'You *did* come with him, didn't you?'

'Dr Clancy?' Tricia tried to free her tongue and
speak normally, but the words came in a high
squeak. 'I came by taxi,' she said.

'I hope he knows that. We were anxious about
you girls when we heard the news that a maniac was
trying to pick up nurses. He dropped everything to
make sure you all returned safely, and used his own
car. I'd hate to think he scoured the West End of
London fearing you'd been abducted, Nurse.'

Tricia looked away, unable to meet the steely gaze
that still had the glint of a hospital nursing officer,
although the lady had been retired for six years and
now worked for the Charity Commission.

'It's all right, Mrs Monteroy. I brought back three
nurses, and I see that one came back safely alone,'
the remembered voice announced, and Tricia turned
to see a tall figure, with broad shoulders filling a
loose tracksuit and long legs tapering from taut hips.

'Any trouble?' asked Mrs Monteroy, taking the
boxes from the other nurses, who eyed Tricia with a
mixture of amusement and malice.

He ran a hand through his hair and looked directly at the girl facing him. 'Not really trouble, unless you count being stopped by the police and having to rely on these nurses to assure them that I am a doctor here, with a spotless reputation with women, so I'm not a rapist. They had a description of me that was a bit like a passport picture taken in a cheap booth, and my hair is *not* ginger as described by one timid mouse who refused my lift.'

'I never said it was,' whispered Tricia.

'That's what the man had written in his little notebook, I believe. Remind me to get a haircut,' he said to nobody in particular. 'He said it was untidy. What a way to be described in my new police dossier!'

Tricia ventured to glance at his face. The mouth was set in a firm line as if to intimidate her, but the eyes held a glow that came from suppressed laughter. She blushed. Tomorrow the whole of Beattie's would know about the stupid first-year nurse who nearly had Dr Clancy arrested.

'I have a message for all the nurses who were out collecting today. It's not worth changing into clean uniform now, so you may all have the rest of the day off,' Sister Ruth King, the Casualty and Outpatients sister, said as she walked up to the group and gave a sweet smile to Dr Clancy. 'You poor dear, I've made coffee in my office. You just *must* take time for some. I thought you were off duty today, and yet you seem to have been working for the hospital all day.'

'Thanks, Ruth, I need it to soothe my shattered

nerves,' he grinned. 'And my shattered ego. I
thought everyone here knew me, but obviously I've
made no impression on some people.'

'Are you Nurse Metcalf?' asked Sister King. Tricia
nodded, wondering what more could happen to her.
'She's first-year and only just out of Block after the
past month, and you've been here only three weeks,'
Sister explained, as if Nurse Metcalf was not there
or was unable to make her own excuses. 'Her friend
told me just now, when I bandaged her ankle.'

'How is she?' Tricia asked impulsively, then wondered if she ought to wait until she was spoken to,
as they were talking over her head as if she wasn't
there!

'Fine. She can go on duty tomorrow, but she must
take it easy, which won't be difficult with all the staff
you seem to have up there. She had physio and has
gone down to have tea. I said I'd tell you.' She
seemed quite friendly but Tricia decided that Sister
Ruth King was, as Josie suggested, intent on keeping
Dr Clancy all to herself and could afford to be
pleasant now that she knew there was no threat from
the quiet dark-haired girl who seemed frightened of
his shadow. 'I might ask Sister Stafford to lend me
someone for the big orthopaedic clinic tomorrow.
Maybe you, Nurse Metcalf.' Sister touched the doctor's arm in a familiar way. 'Coffee and sympathy,'
she suggested.

'First I must buy a rose,' he said. 'I've been very
much involved with them this afternoon and I really
must have one as a reminder not to speak to strange
women. I know now what trouble they can cause.'

Sister Ruth laughed and turned away to make sure the coffee was ready, and he advanced to the table, put money in a box and handed a rose to Tricia. Dumbly she took it and peeled away the paper backing, then placed it firmly over his heart on the green tracksuit. He held her hand briefly. 'Cheer up,' he said softly. 'Worse things happen at sea. You look like my youngest sister when she's in trouble.' His hand was firm and gentle, and she wanted to press it to her cheek and ask for—what? Forgiveness? Or friendship? Or something that she knew could never be hers: the approval and affection of this dynamic man.

CHAPTER TWO

THE row of faces seemed endless and the list of new patients that Sister King put up on the board even worse. 'It's going to be busy,' Sister King said with satisfaction. She put a pile of notes from local GPs on the desk. 'Your job will be to fetch the patients I call for, find the notes and X-rays and deliver them to me in the consultant's cubicle that you find empty.'

'Yes, Sister,' Tricia replied, and was glad to be given something simple to do, but some of the patients were in wheelchairs and some on stretcher trolleys and the cubicles were small, so it took time to get one in before the consultant finished examining the one next door.

She found too that notes had a curious habit of disappearing just when they were needed, mostly due to the house surgeon's taking them and not bringing them back in time, and some patients had been X-rayed on the way in after accidents and the pictures were still in the X-ray department.

Some patients wore plaster casts of varying degrees of heaviness, and others came in limping with the aid of elbow crutches or sticks, and the old patients, in for checks or removal of plaster, waited patiently for the house surgeon to see them.

Tricia smiled as she saw a man wearing a leg

plaster disappear behind a screen, followed by a determined-looking HS wearing a long plastic apron and carrying an enormous pair of plaster shears. She stifled a giggle. He was like a comedian in a sketch pretending to do unimaginable horrors to a pretend patient on an operating table. Fifteen minutes later they emerged, the X-rays were checked and the man beamed as he scratched his bare leg with all the pleasure a dog showed when rolling in grass.

He saw the smiling nurse. 'Cor, I've wanted to do that for weeks! Nearly lost a knitting needle down the plaster trying to get to the itch, and now I can have a bath and feel human.' He sniffed. 'Bit niffy after all this time, but I'm not going home by bus.'

'Come for a check-up in six weeks, or before that if you have problems, otherwise see your GP,' the HS told him. 'Go easy for a while and the muscles may need a bit of gentle exercise in Physio, but no strain, and don't drive like that again. That tibia wasn't a pretty sight in the first X-ray!'

'I've got a lift home, and it will be good to be comfortable at my desk again. That plaster got in the way of tables and chairs and was hell in bed! Thanks for everything, and I hope I never see you all again,' the man added, laughing.

Sister King hurried in and out of the various cubicles, checking notes and making sure that neither of the two consultants was kept waiting, and the flow of patients went smoothly until lunchtime. From time to time, a patient was sent up to the orthopaedic ward for admission, and twice Tricia

was sent up, pushing a wheelchair patient, trying to
manage the notes and X-rays at the same time.

'Bloody nuisance,' she heard as she closed the lift
doors and pushed a young man along to the ward.
She eased the chair gently over the polished corridor, trying to keep it straight, but, like so many
chairs and supermarket trolleys, it seemed to want
to go in every direction but the one required. 'Sorry,
Nurse, but I'm so mad at myself for doing this.' The
young man's face was pale and his eyes glittered
with mixed pain and anger.

'At least you can be sure of good treatment, and
you'll soon be home again,' she ventured.

'Soon?' He gave a shout of derision, then seemed
to catch his breath sharply. 'Soon, she says! Do you
know how long it was that my father was in hospital
for a cartilage op? Six ruddy weeks, that's all, and
the next trials are in a month's time!'

'I don't think they take as long now,' she said.
'What happened, Mr Bradley?'

'Mister? You make me feel a hundred. Ivor will
do.' He eyed her with sudden approval as if he was
only then aware that she was a girl and pretty. 'We
must be about the same age, and she calls me
Mister!'

'Well, I'm Nurse Metcalf on duty,' she said
demurely. 'Hospital rules. You still haven't said how
it happened, and I haven't read your notes.'

'You haven't seen the pictures? I won a canoe
slalom championship last year and hoped to repeat
it this time.' His arrogance faded. 'Oh, God! You've
never heard of me and nobody else will remember

me if I don't get it right again and soon. I was practising on the River Wye in white water and hit a submerged rock. I went over and should have come full circle, but a branch caught my arm and pulled me clear. Crunch!' he added morosely. 'Another rock and one knee kaput.'

'I'm really sorry,' was all that Tricia could say.

'I'm afraid you'll have to go to Men's Surgical,' the sister said when they arrived at the orthopaedic ward door. 'We've had news of an accident on a building site and three men have been dug out with query back injuries, so we must save the beds for *real* cases. I rang Sister Stafford and she said she'll take you.'

'There's fame for you!' Ivor Bradley grinned for the first time. 'Not a proper case? She has no idea of the agony. Really cuts a guy down to size. Picture in four papers last year, and I can't even get into the right ward now!'

'You'll like Sister Stafford,' Tricia told him, and when she pushed open the ward door, Josie greeted them.

'Finished with you already?' she asked.

'No, just bringing Ivor Bradley for admission,' said Tricia. 'Do I have to wait and see Sister, or do you take him?'

'Sister said I was to make him get into bed and be ready for examination.'

'I've been prodded and pulled around enough!' Ivor protested.

'This is different.' Tricia nearly dropped the notes as she heard that voice again. 'I shall be giving you your anaesthetic and I want to go over your chest and check your blood pressure,' said Dr Clancy. 'Any objection to getting this done soon? Like tomorrow morning at eight-thirty?'

'No kidding?' Ivor's face cleared. 'Then how long after that, Doc?'

Dr Clancy held out a hand to Tricia. 'X-rays, Nurse.'

She fumbled for the big envelope between the notes and dropped it. 'Sorry,' she said in a chastened voice, but her hands were shaking. The envelope was scooped up in a firm grasp and the flap opened with no comment from the doctor. She sensed his hidden impatience and bit her lip. I'm not really such a fool, she wanted to say, but it was obvious that to him she was a real idiot.

'Can't keep away from surgery, Mr Clancy?' Sister Stafford sounded amused. 'I don't know why you aren't here as a surgeon. Any other doctor with a Fellowship of the Royal College of Surgeons would be down there in a gown and mask, wielding a scalpel, not going over perfectly fit chests with a stethoscope, like a second-year student, and calling himself Doctor.'

'I just like to know what's happening at the other end of the table,' he replied mildly. 'Especially if there's any chance of my patient turning blue. I know that any doctor can give a basic anaesthetic, but it's become such a complicated science that when I find myself on a desert island with a man with a burst appendix and I have to do both the gas and the operation, I want him asleep!'

Ivor laughed, and Tricia felt that the mild amused exchange between Dr Clancy and Sister Stafford was deliberately meant to make him relax. Certainly the white knuckles no longer gripped the arms of the wheelchair and he had more colour in his face, although he still breathed quickly.

'On a desert island all you'd need would be a mallet to knock him out and one rusty knife,' he said, with a ghoulish grin. 'Not much science; or some of the tapes they play on *Desert Island Discs* would be enough to send anyone to sleep.'

'Nice pictures,' Dr Clancy said with approval. 'Not a big tear in the cartilage, and I think they'll remove the fragment through a very tiny hole, by remote control, you could say. After physio, of which we have the best at Beattie's, you should be mobile in a week or so at most.'

'Let's go, then! Which bed, Nurse?'

Josie Allen pushed Ivor behind the drawn curtains at the far end of the ward, and Sister turned to her other junior nurse.

'You can put the notes down in my office, Nurse Metcalf, and go back to Sister King if she still needs you. Report back to me before you go off duty— and for heaven's sake, girl, stop looking so worried! He'll be fine. I supppose he told you a great old tale about how he was fished out of the water unconscious and had to be given the kiss of life, and was taken to the local cottage hospital? Then he was transferred at speed with ambulance bells clanging to Gloucester until he was over the first shock and chill, where the surgeon suggested Mr Attril of

Beattie's as the man most likely to give him a workable knee again? It's a long way from Wales and he's over-tired and over-stimulated.'

She looked at Dr Clancy, who was regarding Tricia with a faint air of puzzled amusement. 'I think they had no right to transfer him just now, so if you'd write him up for a sedative I think he ought to sleep through,' she added to Dr Clancy.

He followed Tricia into the office and sat at the desk, selected a prescription pad and wrote up the sedative, then made notes on the chart as to the premedication that Ivor Bradley would be given early the next morning to relax him for the operation. 'Incidentally, that was all true,' he told her. 'He really had trouble in that river.'

'He said nothing about that to me,' Tricia replied.

'I thought not. I have a feeling he's hiding something so that he can get out of here quickly. I must make sure he has no other injuries, as he told the ambulance crew that he'd just a bashed knee and hoped to go in for a big race next month, but his pulse isn't good and he was unconscious for longer than we like to see. He insisted that he wasn't a stretcher case and put up with a wheelchair that must have been fairly uncomfortable. I'll give him five minutes to get his breath before I examine him thoroughly. Done any Theatre?' he asked casually.

'No. . .sir.'

'"No, Dr Clancy" will do,' he said, and the firm mouth twitched at the corners. 'However, a bit of respect restores my deflated ego. What do they call you at home?' He was busy writing, and Tricia gulped. 'Not Miss Metcalf, I presume?'

'Patricia,' she said, and he smiled. He put the notes on the desk, neatly, with the chart on top, and swung the chair round to face her, then got up and loomed over her, his hair flopping over one brow until he pushed impatient fingers through it. She was breathlessly aware of him, and the room seemed to shrink as she backed away.

'Surely not Patricia? You haven't the nose for that name. Much too small and kissable. More like a Tricia or a Trixie; not even Pat.' He bent and for a second his lips brushed the tip of her nose as if he held a puppy. 'I have a sister Trixie,' he said, and strode from the office.

For a moment, Tricia clung to the desk, then she walked slowly to the door, ready to go back to Outpatients. His kiss had been friendly and even affectionate, but no more, yet her pulse quickened and her eyes held a soft expression. Nobody had ever called her Trixie, and she fervently hoped he could see the difference between her and his sister.

The door caught her elbow as it was flung back and Dr Clancy strode back into the office, demanding his stethoscope as if it had been her fault that he'd mislaid it. 'Hurry up! Emergency! I haven't got all day,' he snapped. The neat pile of notes was scattered and he picked up the instrument, running back to the ward and disappearing behind the curtains where Ivor was now in bed.

Dahlia hurried in and unlocked the drug cupboard door, grabbed a phial and syringes and hurried out again. 'Get back to Outpatients, Nurse,' she called over her shoulder. 'There are too many of us here as it is!'

Tricia tidied the office desk, rescued a pen that had fallen on the floor from one torn pocket in Dr Clancy's white coat, rubbed her sore elbow and walked back to Outpatients, feeling incompetent and unwanted.

'Nurse, we need the notes of Mrs Briony Meek from Gynae. If they're not there, try Records, but she was discharged from Gynae yesterday and the notes might still be there,' Sister King said as soon as Tricia reported back to Outpatients. She laughed. 'What bad luck! She went home and the next day she tripped over the cat, so back she came with a broken wrist.'

'Is she to be admitted, Sister? I remember her from Gynae before we went into Block. She had a D & C and they were waiting for the results before deciding what to do next.'

'She had a cold, so they put off her other op, and she had that last week.' Sister King looked at her keenly. 'You liked her?'

'She was very nice, and we all hoped that the path report wouldn't show up something bad,' Tricia said.

'That's why I must check her notes carefully. I have no idea if she's on any medication, and if she has to go to Theatre, the anaesthetist must know so that he can gear his injections to whatever she needs that doesn't clash with her own drugs.'

'Will they have to take her to Theatre, Sister? Why not plaster?' asked Tricia.

'The X-rays show a splinter that might have to be removed, and Mr Attril will decide once I have her notes, but we alerted the theatre in case she has to have the wrist reduced under anaesthetic.' A porter handed Sister a memo. 'Oh, good, I asked the lab for details of her gynae scrape and it was innocent, but they recommended a hysterectomy to stop the enormous periods she's suffered for years. The tablets she talks about could be a vitamin and iron supplement, of course, to make up for years of chronic anaemia from blood loss, but she refers to "them little white pills", which could be anything!'

'Who would give the anaesthetic?' Tricia asked with an air of innocence. I must be out of my mind, she thought. I just want to hear about him or even just to make someone say his name.

'There are several. Dr Boris Pilatzcech is in overall charge. Been here for ages and married a Beattie's nurse. Everyone lusts after him, even if his hair is greying very romantically at the temples, but he never looks at another woman and adores his wife. He has several lesser bods who finish his major lists after he's given anaesthetics for any transplants and anything to do with heart-lung surgery.' Tricia waited expectantly.

'The ENT men like to have their own doctors who understand micro-surgery and how to keep the head clear of tubes on the side where they want to operate.' Ruth King smiled and suddenly looked very pretty. 'Then there's Dr Clancy, whom you met today. He's a sweetie and a very dear personal friend. He's doing six months here under Dr Boris in case he wants to settle in some backwoods area in Canada where his sister Jenny lives, but he came from a big accident hospital in the Midlands.'

'Jenny? I thought her name was Trixie,' queried Tricia.

'That's another sister. I was at school with her and know all the family. Jenny's a computer operator and got married last year and moved to Canada.' Ruth King eyed Tricia curiously. 'You sounded as if you know the family.'

'No,' Tricia said hastily. 'He just mentioned a sister called Trixie, that's all.'

Ruth King's eyes narrowed. 'When did you discuss his family? He doesn't often talk about his private affairs. You only saw him for five minutes here. Of course—you were the one who got him in trouble with the police!' She broke into peals of laughter in which there was a hint of relief. 'He'll never forgive you,' she said with satisfaction, and noticed that the junior nurse went red and looked very chastened.

The notes were hard to find, but eventually Tricia brought them back to Outpatients, where the last of the patients was sitting with leg outstretched on a chair waiting for the plaster to dry enough to go home by ambulance.

Sister King studied the papers, and Tricia admired her calm efficiency, even though she knew it meant that Ruth King could get and keep the man she had known for a long time, and whom she treated with easy familiarity. How could an inexperienced nurse with hang-ups compare with a woman like her who had so much to offer a man in the medical profession and who was already a part of his private life?

Mr Attril came out of the surgeons' shower-room, scraping plaster from under his fingernails. 'I must leave plasters to my registrar or house surgeon, he said testily, then grinned. 'I sometimes think they have all the fun and I have the worry, but I was very proud of my plasters when I was an HS and I can't resist doing the twiddly bits if I see a rough edge.' He turned and smiled. 'Ah, there you are, Clancy. Don't think I'll need you after all. I hope I didn't upset your schedule by keeping you waiting for Mrs Meek?'

He sat by the desk and examined the notes and X-rays of the fractured wrist. 'I think she can get by with a plaster, but she's a heavy woman and we can't make it too light in case she falls about again on it.' He looked at the old notes. 'Not the first time she's been here, but that was for severe bruising and nothing actually broken. Seems to be a bit accident-prone.'

Dr Clancy looked at the notes. 'Why did she fall this time?' he asked.

'The cat got under her feet, or so she thinks, but she can't really remember,' said Ruth King. 'I don't think she had a blackout, but if she didn't remember, how can we tell what really happened?'

'Have we a bed?' asked Dr Clancy. 'I'd like to keep her in overnight and ask the medical firm to look at her. I know this lady as I was there when they took out her uterus.'

'If you think so, fine,' Mr Attril said. 'As far as

I'm concerned the wrist can be plastered and she can go home, but I saw her only today. Ring through, Sister, and I'll get Harris to plaster the wrist and tell her she needs a rest here while it sets.'

'Thank you,' said Dr Clancy. 'No need to alarm her, but I see she's been put on Thyroxine since her operation, and as you know, Nurse,' he said, looking directly at Tricia, 'that indicates that she had a thyroid deficiency called myxoedema. Quite a lot of people get it without realising it. Everything slows down and the reaction to even simple things isn't fast enough. People become clumsy.'

She blushed, aware that under the real information he was teasing her, and she was goaded into saying, 'Sister Stafford thought so when Mrs Meek came in for her first investigation.' She spoke in a clear voice. 'She even mentioned Thyroxine and said she'd suggest that a medical team should examine her. She said the coarse skin was a typical symptom too,' she added, aware that he was looking with great interest at her clear fresh complexion—or had she a spot on her cheek?

'Good for you,' he said, laughing. 'Never underestimate the knowledge of a first-year nurse.' But she had the impression that he reluctantly admired the way she had answered back. 'Now tell me why I want her checked, if as you say she might have had treatment,' he said with a scary frown.'

Sister King was amused by the sudden panic in the girl's wide eyes. 'Don't tease her,' she said indulgently.

'Mrs Meek had her uterus removed and one

ovary, as there was a benign cyst on it,' he explained. 'That means it was harmless but might grow bigger. The thyroid stimulates the other hormonal glands to produce the right substances to keep the body working well, but her thyroid wasn't efficient, and may not have been for years, making her balance of hormones wrong.'

Tricia nodded and forgot her own embarrassment in the interest she discovered in his explanation. 'If the ovaries aren't functioning well and then the thyroid is upset by sudden doses of what amounts to extra power, it might have a see-saw effect when she exerts herself too much,' he went on. 'I want her to have a test to see if the right dosage is being given. If it's correct, then I accept that the cat was to blame for her fall. In time the drug will give her energy and a new enjoyment of life, but at first we need caution.'

He laughed. 'I may be a surgeon, and an anaesthetist at least for a while, but as in all medicine, one skill meets another skill, and we all have to be physicians too, under the skin.'

Was he boasting or just making a modest excuse for knowing so much? Tricia wondered. He'd be marvellous in the lecture-room. She for one would never go to sleep while he was talking. He picked up a bulging briefcase from which papers stuck out by the hasps and followed Sister King into her office, but came out again almost at once, although Tricia knew that coffee was percolating ready for him whenever he happened to appear.

Dr Clancy went to the internal phone to take a

call. 'Right,' he said crisply. 'Sounds interesting, Boris. Yes, I'd like to sit in and observe.' He walked quickly to the door, then turned. 'Tell Sister I can't make it. I shall be in Theatre and I have no idea for how long, so. . .another time, perhaps?' He gave her a smile of such sweetness that Tricia felt nerveless, and yet she had to brace herself to tell Sister King that her date with Dr Clancy was off.

'Damn! He promised me he'd drive me to Dorking this evening to see friends,' complained Sister.

'It must be disappointing for both of you, Sister,' Tricia said tactfully, 'but this must happen all the time, I suppose. I had no idea just how much nursing would affect one's social life.'

'They're my friends,' Ruth King confessed. 'I wanted to introduce him to them, but each time he's made some excuse. I told him they know Trixie and that seemed to make a difference, so I thought it was safe to ring them to say we'd be over for coffee about eight. I don't drive, so that means I have to put them off. It's too bad!' Her mouth took on a petulant slant and Tricia glimpsed the bad temper that could erupt at any moment.

'I have to go back and report to Sister Stafford,' she said hurriedly, and escaped.

'What happened?' she demanded when she got to the ward. The bed where Ivor had been taken for examination was empty, the bedding rolled back to one side and the pillows stacked on a chair.

'He was rushed off to Theatre,' Josie told her. 'I nearly got killed in the hassle. Help me make the bed up as a post-op bed. Sister threatens to see if we learned anything in Block.'

'But why the sudden rush to Theatre? Did Dr Clancy know about it?' Tricia recalled how he had hurried from the office with the stethoscope and Staff Nurse Dahlia Stephens had hastily fetched stimulating drugs from the cupboard, but when he was in Outpatients soon after he was calm and even laughed, so she was sure there hadn't been a serious crisis in Ward Seven.

'Of course he knew, fathead. He was here, wasn't he? He examined Ivor and found that a cracked rib had damaged one lung, and as he tapped to find out if there was a pneumo-thorax, Ivor collapsed.'

'A pneumo what?' queried Tricia.

'You know, when air gets into the wrong place in a lung,' Josie said vaguely. 'Between the layers of tissue, he said, and a piece of bone may be embedded, so they can't just treat him here.'

'But he was so unconcerned down in Outpatients,' said Tricia. 'He was even laughing! Doesn't he care?' She recalled his untidy briefcase, his haphazard way of dressing and his longish hair. Was he careless about patients? About people in general? She also remembered that he had seemed amused that he had to leave Sister King on her own when they had a date, as if it was very unimportant.

'I like him,' Josie insisted. 'He moved fast and handed Ivor over to the theatre and the team who were going to cope with him very quickly. By sheer chance, a heart bypass had just been finished and Dr Boris was still in the building, so he took over the anaesthetic as he's used to the thoracic surgeon here.'

'Dr Clancy didn't mention it when he came down to see Mr Attril,' Tricia said.

'He rushed off as soon as he knew Ivor was being taken over with all due care,' said Josie patiently. 'He was expected in another theatre with Mr Attril, Sister said, and he couldn't just leave that and go with Ivor.'

'Mr Attril did say he wouldn't need him after all,' Tricia agreed. Her face cleared. 'Someone rang to ask him to watch an operation, so he must be in the theatre now with Ivor.'

'There! I'm very proud of that,' beamed Josie, regarding the post-op bed with pride. The sheets and blankets were folded up at the sides instead of being tucked in, so that the returning patient could be lifted into the bed quickly with no tangle of clothes to get in the way, and then be covered and tucked in.

'Good,' said Sister Stafford. 'Now make it up normally with fresh linen, as he won't be coming back here for a while. I assume he'll go to Intensive Care or at least to the resuscitation ward.'

'*Well*!' said Josie in a breathy whisper that could be heard all over the ward. 'What a waste of a perfectly good bed!' She folded a sheet. 'I hoped he'd be back here. Quite a dish when he's well, I imagine.'

'Watch it, Josie! You know we mustn't get involved with patients, and I thought you had a boyfriend.'

Sister Stafford made a round of the ward and told the new nurses to change the water in the covered carafes on the bed tables and make a note of the amount of fluid drunk by those on fluid intake and output measurements. 'I like to have the ward straight before Visitors this evening, and I just hope that one of the doctors doesn't have the bright idea to do a round and mess up the beds again,' she said. She looked at the ward clock and sighed. 'I hate this inaction, and after that little bit of excitement we're slack again. You may go off early, Nurses. Make sure the sluice is tidy and the laundry chute is clear and go to late tea-break, then off duty.'

'I suppose one day I shall be a nurse again,' sighed Josie. 'But at the moment, I seem to be encouraged to stay away from patients, not nurse them. Yesterday it was the flag day, and now a ward nearly empty and far from busy. At least it's given my ankle time to recover completely, but I don't think I'll play squash tonight or anything very energetic.'

Tricia looked out of the window and up at the sky. 'While it's light and the sun is good on the trees, I think I'll take a camera to Dulwich Park—that is if you'll come on the bus with me? I hate walking in parks alone, but I do want to take pictures of the lovely rhododendrons that must be coming out about now. I hear they're superb.'

'Do you take many pictures?' asked Josie.

'It's a hobby that started when I was in school and my parents sent me loads of snaps to keep in touch, and I sent them school photos and some when I was on holiday at half-term, too far away to join them in the Med or wherever they were.'

'Do they still send them?'

'Yes, and we all look forward to the exchange. I want to show them that London isn't just a concrete jungle where their dear daughter will be raped, mugged or robbed.'

'Worse still,' said Josie, and laughed, 'you might fall in love with some thoroughly unsuitable man!'

'Not a hope!' Tricia declared with far too much vehemence, and Josie regarded her with interest.

'You saw him too?'

'Who?'

'The Casualty Officer. Dreamy, with a look of Sting about him, but shorter hair. He's called Paul Jeffrey and he's been here for over a year.'

'I haven't seen him. He wasn't in Outpatients today, but I think he was in Minor Ops all morning doing small cases under local anaesthetics.' Tricia smiled. 'We heard yells at one time, and Sister shrugged and said he wasn't as gentle as he might be at times if the patient didn't co-operate.'

'I like my men a bit mean and macho,' said Josie. 'He looks almost lazy and very sexy, but he deals with the Saturday night yobs very successfully. You should see his biceps!'

'Maybe you'd like his picture?' teased Tricia, and hurried to change and fetch her camera.

The park was almost empty and at one end of the first avenue the trees were only in bud, but further along, where the sun shone on them for most of the day, the delicate flowers burst out in a rainbow of colours.

'Great,' Tricia said for the third time, and walked quickly towards a particularly fine crimson-flowered tree. 'I'll take one of you now,' she called, and checked her light meter. 'Hurry up, the light's going. Stand over there.'

She heard a giggle as she bent over the camera, and froze as she focused the view-finder. In the small aperture were two figures, one of Josie and the other of a man, standing beside her, grinning. Instinctively she released the shutter, then looked up. Dr Clancy came forward, and she saw that from his neck hung a very expensive camera.

'Snap,' he said. 'Or is that a very weak pun?'

'What are you doing here?' she asked inanely.

'The same as you. Not many people bother with parks, but I love them, and I promised my sister to take some pictures for her to use in a travel brochure that she's been asked to compile. Less of "Come to the Tower of London" and more of "See the real London and the beautiful flowers and trees." She's very good and has bright ideas.'

'Trixie?' suggested Tricia. 'Or Jenny?'

'No, this one is Kate, and no, you aren't a bit like her.'

'How many sisters have you?' asked Josie.

'Four,' he admitted with a smile. 'All different but all very pretty.'

'And they spoil you rotten, I suppose? Tidy up after you and wait on you?' said Tricia, trying to sound ironic. 'Sister said you were spoiled and never put anything away.'

'There are things that matter and things that don't. You should see my anaesthetic-room when I'm working. It's a model of neatness and efficiency. It has to be,' he added seriously, then pushed back the hair over his brow. 'Coming back, or are you still scared of accepting lifts?'

Tricia took the full roll from her camera and sealed it ready to be developed. 'The local chemist does them quite well,' she said. 'I want them soon to send away.'

'I'll leave it in with mine,' Dr Clancy said, and firmly took it from her. 'Sit in the back and rest your ankle, Nurse,' he said to Josie, and Tricia found herself sitting close to him in the front seat.

'Would you leave the ticket for my film in the lodge for me?' she said. 'I can't collect them without it.'

'I'll see you on Ward Seven,' he replied. 'You *will* be there tomorrow?' His hand rested on her arm for a moment, sending shafts of pleasure through her body.

'Have you a case there?' she asked.

'I don't need a case to visit Sister Stafford,' he replied enigmatically. He took them to the main entrance, drove down to the lodge to collect a parcel and left the girls to go to supper. Sister King watched them get out of the car, and her face was white with fury. It was only seven o'clock and there would have been plenty of time to visit her friends if he had left a message for her, instead of taking two of the new nurses out in his car.

CHAPTER THREE

'I'M NOT off tonight. Sister Stafford thinks we may have cases from the afternoon clinic, so I'm off this morning after my coffee break. It's two days since Dr Clancy left the films in to be developed and I want to see if they're ready. I can go there this morning.' Tricia tucked the sheet in tightly and smoothed the bedcover.

'I have a date this evening, so Dahlia managed to get Sister to let me have the evening off,' said Josie complacently. 'She doesn't act like any staff nurse I've heard about. She's nice.'

'If we're to be busy, I'd rather stay. I'm better if I'm stretched hard as there isn't time to be frightened,' Tricia confessed.

'You can't be frightened of anyone here. Sister's OK and the doctors are a fairly mild bunch, except for Mr Masters, the general surgeon. I saw him in the corridor surrounded by a bevy of students and he was being very sarcastic to one of them, poor lad.'

'Fortunately we're far too junior to be in much contact with him. He has Sister and Staff Nurse with him when he makes a round and we just follow and tidy up after them,' said Tricia.

The ward was quiet and there were at least ten

empty beds in the twenty-bed unit, the pretty curtains separating the beds were pulled back and the matching bedspreads looked clean and fresh and very innocent, as if there had never been men in pain occupying the calm cubicles.

The ward cleaner slowly pushed a damp cloth along a ridge on one of the wooden partitions that made four-bed units, dividing the big ward, and the second-year nurse brought a trolley of flower vases filled with freshly arranged flowers, ready to be distributed as soon as the locker tops had been wiped.

Staff Nurse Dahlia Stephens handed out morning drugs and told Tricia exactly what use they had. 'Mr Davies had had a stomach ulcer that didn't get better just with diet and the usual anti-acid remedies like magnesium tricilicate, and he had a reaction to stronger drugs, so it was decided to take away a part of his stomach. He gets a little discomfort after surgery, but needs only a mild sedative at night now, and we take samples of his stomach juices each morning to see how he's responding to rest and light diet after his op last week.'

'Does that tube stay in all the time?' Tricia asked.

They walked to his bedside. 'You aren't bothered by that tube, are you, Mr Davies?'

'Not really, if it's necessary to have it, Nurse.'

Nurse Stephens beamed. 'That's what I like to hear. Mr Davies is my model patient, so he gets well fast!' She carefully fitted a large syringe to the end of the Ryle's tube which was strapped to his cheek and going down inside his nose into the stomach.

She withdrew a few cc of straw-coloured fluid and put it in a test tube which Tricia sealed and labelled with his name, the time and date and what it contained, and put it in a rack with other specimens for the path lab. 'Great,' Dahlia said, and her patient smiled. 'Not a trace of blood, and if Mr Masters gives permission we might have that tube out today.'

'Does that mean he can be discharged, Nurse?' Tricia looked at the empty beds.

'Another empty bed? Yes, we get slack sometimes at half-term when the schools are out. Parents put off coming in for ops if they aren't urgent so that they can be with their families. It happens when they want to go away on holiday and again at the main Easter and Christmas breaks, but the poor hospitals by the sea and other holiday spots get more than their fair share at those times if an emergency arises! Maybe the whole country is getting healthy and we shall be out of work!' Dahlia's ample shoulders shook with laughter. 'That'll be the day,' she added.

Tricia was on her way to the office to ask if she could go down for coffee and off-duty, when the ward door swung back to admit Mr Masters.

'Sister about?' he asked abruptly. 'I'm in a hurry. My list has started and I can't leave my registrar for more than the first two hernias.' Sister Stafford came to meet him. 'Don't you ever work on this ward?' he asked, with a kind of grim humour, looking at the empty beds. 'Is it only the women who come to me for surgery now? I have two femoral hernias today, both from Women's Surgical, a female thyroid and a couple of partial gastrectomies.'

'We might be busy tomorrow,' Sister said. She went into the office to collect the relevant charts, and the surgeon shifted from one foot to the other impatiently.

'Nurse, get me a kidney dish and a swab or two,' he demanded, and Tricia fled to the clinical-room and came back with them quickly. 'Where's Mr Davies?'

Tricia gave one agonised glance towards the office, where through the frosted glass panel she could see Sister talking on the telephone, holding a handful of notes ready for Mr Masters but unable to leave the phone. Mr Masters frowned and she hurried to pull the cubicle curtains round the patient, hoping against hope that Sister or Staff Nurse would rescue her.

'Better?' he asked, and Mr Davies smiled. Tricia was amazed at the sudden gentleness of the probing fingers as they explored the abdomen round the rapidly healing scar. 'We'll relieve you of that tube,' Mr Masters said. 'Nurse?'

'Yes, sir?'

'Take off the strapping on the cheek. Now I understand that you know a lot about manor houses, Mr Davies? A colleague of mine comes from a small manor in Devon. Still in the family, I believe, but thinking of selling up. Pity, but it happens. Nice to think of the same families living in them for hundreds of years.'

Mr Davies relaxed and his eyes shone. 'Do you recall the name, Mr Masters?'

The surgeon turned away for a moment, long

enough to say quietly, 'Nurse, you can withdraw that tube very firmly but slowly, without stopping midway. Do it now.'

'But, sir——!'

'Do it.' He turned back to the patient. 'Does Knoll Barton mean anything to you? Now keep quite still.'

Mr Davies smiled. 'Knoll Barton is a very fine example of early English architecture with some Norman remains and a bit of very bad Victorian addition, but it's a pretty place and needs a big family to fill it again, not just to be taken for a conference centre or whatever, as so many have been. I was there only last. . . Oh!' He stared at the slimy piece of rubber tubing with the tiny weight on the perforated end that Tricia held up before she coiled it into the kidney dish. He gulped and then smiled again. 'I hardly noticed what you were doing, Nurse. I was so interested in Knoll Barton that I just didn't even feel sick. I was dreading that tube coming out as I heard it might make me vomit.'

'That will be all, Nurse,' said Mr Masters. 'Don't look so startled! It's all over—and yes, you did it all by yourself! Neither of you suffered much, did you? Sister's coming now to do the easy bits.' He smiled suddenly. 'Thank you.'

Tricia wiped away the mark of the strapping and gave Mr Davies a tissue for his nose, which was running slightly, then took the kidney dish to the clinical-room, where Dahlia was just covering a dressing trolley with a sterile towel. She glanced into the dish at the soggy tube.

'Someone got worms?' she asked, and laughed. 'Who took the tube out?'

'Me!' Tricia told her in a squeaky voice. 'He made me do it! Mr Davies didn't even seem to notice, but it made me feel quite sick.'

'Mr Masters is a bad old tease. He hates to do it himself and chooses the most junior nurse around to help him if he can get away with it. He says the more frightened you are the more careful you become, and he could be right. Soak it in bicarbonate of soda solution to get rid of the mucus and I'll syringe it through later and sterilise it. Now get off before he makes you help him in Theatre!'

Tricia changed into a bodystocking of deep blue and a tiny skirt of a lighter blue that toned with the jacket of stone-washed denim. A big light 'throw' of tawny wool covered her shoulders, and her flat shoes of dark tan were old and comfortable as she swung easily along the driveway with a duffle handbag slung over one arm. The sun was capricious, hiding behind a cloud and then bursting out with such warmth that she wished she had worn something lighter, but she dared not take off her jacket out of doors as she knew that the bodystocking was a bit revealing where the close fit followed every curve of her anatomy.

The small boutique was in the process of having the window changed, and she saw summer dresses stacked ready to fit the models. Suddenly her clothes felt out of season, almost wintry, and she stopped to look in the shop at the packed rails of pretty and inexpensive clothes. Reluctantly she dragged herself away to do more serious shopping and filled her duffel with chocolate and biscuits, ready for a visit to a friend with children. She examined a new range of cosmetics, approving the fact that they were made without experimenting on animals, and bought a new lipstick of soft browny-rose.

A frantic rummage inside her bag showed her that she had not brought the ticket she had to show to receive her prints. 'Damn,' she said softly. It meant going back to her room to fetch it.

'Lost a prescription?' the assistant asked.

'Nothing serious,' Tricia said with a forced smile. 'Dr Clancy left some films to be developed and I wondered if they were ready, but I've left the slip in my room.'

'Dr Clancy came in earlier and they hadn't arrived, but they came in ten minutes ago and you can take them. He had a slip,' the girl added. 'In fact he left it on the counter and I put it with the films.'

'But not my slip. It was two separate orders,' Tricia insisted.

'Not to worry. I can put his on his bill as he ordered some more film that we hadn't in stock, and you can take them both now as he said he wanted them quickly. Just pay for your own and check that they're the right prints before you leave the shop,' the assistant suggested.

Tricia sighed. The girl obviously thought she and Dr Clancy were good friends if not more! I don't even know where he lives, she thought, and decided she would leave the prints in the porter's lodge and a message that they were there to be picked up.

She glanced through the prints and smiled at some she had almost forgotten she had taken. The ones taken in the park were good, and she lingered over the one of Josie and Dr Clancy until the girl said in a rather impatient voice, 'Check the others to make sure they're right.'

Tricia opened the pack and tried not to look too closely, as she felt they were private. She stopped suddenly. There was a very good photograph of herself, holding her camera and about to take snaps of the plants in the park. Her cheeks glowed. 'What a cheek!' she exclaimed. 'He must have been watching us for ages!'

She pushed them back inside the envelope and paid for her own prints, then left hurriedly. Why me? she thought. He must have a warped sense of humour to sneak up on people and take pictures like that. She calmed down. Maybe he would offer her a print and grin in that disarming way to tease her. Just as he might act with his sister, she thought, and found the idea depressing. It was one thing to tease a sister, but quite a different situation when it involved a girl who. . . She blushed. He doesn't even like me, she decided, and he's done nothing to make me really fall for him. One small kiss because I reminded him of Trixie was hardly a turn-on for either of them. I must never confuse a kind of brotherly near-affection for love, she thought firmly.

The lodge window was shut fast, which meant that the porter had gone up to the hospital, either with a parcel urgently needed in one of the departments or to skive off to see his friend in Casualty. Tricia hung about for five minutes, then decided to ask in Casualty if they had seen Dr Clancy.

Timidly, as she was off duty and not in uniform, she ventured into the large hall where outpatients reported for the various clinics or which was used as a fracture clinic during bad weather when Beattie's was overloaded with patients who had slipped on ice and were brought in with broken bones. The room was empty, and the girl in charge of the desk was a medical secretary.

'No outpatients just now, but if you want the casualty officer he's in there,' she said. 'Give me your name first and go in and wait.' Tricia opened her mouth to speak, but the girl was already talking rapidly on the telephone, so she shrugged and walked into the room indicated. A tall man with fair hair was writing up notes. His face was smoothly good-looking, but as he turned to see who had approached the desk, his eyes were very blue with a glint of chill that Tricia found repelling.

'What seems to be the trouble?' he asked, and smiled. 'Nothing, by the look of you.'

'I was looking for Dr Clancy,' she replied. 'I have something for him.'

'Clancy? He isn't with us. I'm Dr Paul Jeffrey, the casualty officer. He comes when I need him to give gas.' He made it sound as if Dr Clancy was his errand boy. 'You are——?'

'Nurse Metcalf,' Tricia told him.

'Pity.' The blue eyes took in every detail of her

long legs and slim hips. 'You mean I can't examine you to find out what the trouble might be?'

'I was asked to give Dr Clancy a message,' she said, 'and if you have no idea where he is, then I'll try the lodge again.'

'If I see him, where can he find you?'

'I work on Ward Seven and I go back on duty after lunch.' She heard voices and realised that the lighter voice was that of Sister Ruth King.

'Ah, Ruth likes to think she keeps tabs on her clever surgeon. Maybe she can help you,' said Dr Jeffrey.

Ruth King came into the room with a junior doctor in tow, and neither looked very happy. 'Dr Mason says he's to give your three gases today, and not Dr Clancy.'

'They're very minor cases and I could easily do them under local, but the pain threshold of some people is pretty low, and they make a fuss,' the casualty officer said.

'Where is he? I want to see him,' said Sister King. 'He hasn't come near my department for two days, and I have something to say to him.' She noticed the junior nurse. 'Nurse Metcalf? What are you doing here out of uniform?'

Paul Jeffrey looked amused. 'Dr Clancy *is* popular! This pretty girl is also waiting to see him.'

'I was asked to bring these for him when I collected my films this morning,' Tricia explained.

'Give them to me,' Sister King commanded. 'If he doesn't come here, I shall go up to Theatre B this afternoon where I know he has at least two big cases, and I can give them to him there.'

Reluctantly, Tricia handed over the packet and left, wondering why Sister King had looked at her as if she hated her. I've done nothing wrong, she thought. Perhaps she's in a mood and treats everyone like that while her bad temper lasts.

She took her films on duty with her to show Josie and Mr Davies, who wanted to see what the Victorian archways were like in the park next to the hospital, in case he wanted a picture for a book he was compiling. 'I'm a librarian,' he explained. 'I know how valuable books like that can be for people needing them for research when they want details of a certain era.'

'I'll have an extra print made if you'd like it,' offered Tricia. 'We have your address in the book, if you've been discharged before it's ready.'

'That one's good,' he said, and Tricia saw she had given him some snaps that she had meant to keep back. 'Could I have one of these too? I'll pay you now and you can send them on. Everyone has been so kind here that this will remind me of you all.'

'Oh, that one!' laughed Tricia. 'It's very good of Nurse Allen, but it's a wonder it isn't a picture of the sky, as I had no idea that Dr Clancy was there until I released the shutter.'

'Is there one of you, Nurse?'

'Sorry, but no. I hate having my picture taken,' she replied.

'Why is that? You're very photogenic,' said Dr Clancy, who had come into the room and now stood

behind her. 'At least I think so, judging by the
negative. Don't tell me you're so camera-shy that
you stole my picture? I thought I'd check with you
before complaining to the shop that I'm one print
short.' He looked faintly annoyed.

'I don't know what you mean,' said Tricia. 'I
collected the pictures and the girl insisted that I
glance at them to see that they were yours, even
when I said I had no idea what subjects you'd used,
but I certainly didn't take one.'

'And you saw the picture I took of you?'

'Yes.'

'If I could have one of those when you find it, I'd
be so grateful,' said Mr Davies. Dr Clancy became
aware of the patient taking in everything that was
said, and dropped his own package of snaps into his
pocket.

'Nothing easier, Mr Davies,' he said quietly. 'At
least I have the negative and this time I'll make sure
I get the prints. Now I want to go over your chest to
make sure you're breathing properly. I gave you
your anaesthetic and you were slightly bubbly afterwards, so a final check before you go home will
make sure you need no more treatment.'

'Shall I fetch Staff Nurse?' asked Tricia.

'No, Nurse Metcalf, you'll do. Sit up, Mr Davies,
and lean forward over Nurse's shoulder. That's
right.'

Gently, the well-shaped hands explored the whole
of the patient's thorax, and gentle fingers tapped
carefully at intervals. Tricia felt the brush of clean
thick hair on her cheek as Dr Clancy bent further to

listen through his stethoscope, as the base of the lungs had not been expanding well before the operation, owing to the pain of the ulcer.

The patient was slight and no real effort was needed to hold him, but Tricia breathed sharply as if she felt those exploring hands on her own body, knowing suddenly that a real man was closer than he needed to be for a simple examination like this. She wanted those hands to caress her and that smile to be only for her, and for him to be lost in an emotion that she longed to share.

'How was that?' Dr Clancy asked the patient, but a pulse beat in his throat and gave the lie to his relaxed voice.

'Fine.' Mr Davies sighed. 'I shall miss being spoiled, and it's been a long time since a pretty girl held me like that.' He chuckled. 'You have very nice shoulders, Nurse.'

'Has she?' Dr Clancy glanced at Tricia as if she was a statue to be viewed. 'You patients get closer than we poor doctors.' He slipped his stethoscope into a deep pocket and looked at the notes. 'You've been given a diet sheet and a list of exercises, I see. I suggest that you dress and walk about the ward and sit in the day-room today, and when your visitors come they can be told to take you home tomorrow after lunch.'

He waited while Tricia tidied the bed and pulled back the curtains, then followed her to the clinical-room. She went to the sink where she had been told to wash instruments from the dressing trolleys, and ran cold water over a dish of forceps that had blood on them, knowing that hot water would only harden the blood but cold water would soon dissolve it. Dr Clancy sat on the edge of a small table that seemed far too fragile for his weight and regarded Tricia with a frown mixed with reluctant humour.

'Well, what have you done with it?' he demanded.

'With what, Dr Clancy?' The wide eyes were startled as she sensed his teasing, and she turned slightly so that he couldn't see her expression.

He left his seat and came up behind her, taking her by the shoulders and shaking her gently. 'A joke's a joke, but I want my property back,' he said. 'What have you done with that photograph?'

'I didn't take it,' she protested, and shook herself free of the restraining hands, turning to face him. She saw the amused expression. 'I did see the picture, but I didn't take it, and what makes you think it's your property? Isn't it an intrusion of privacy to take pictures without the consent of the subject?'

'Come on, give it back. Surely not an intrusion when someone takes a picture of a friend?'

'Friend? If we were friends, you'd know I don't tell lies. Who cares what happened to that picture after I gave them to Sister King? We hardly know each other, Dr Clancy, and if you still think I'm like your sister, then how would she behave now if you accused her of something she hadn't done?' Tricia's lips parted and her cheeks were pink, and she found breathing patchy, her breast heaving with emotion.

'Did I say that?' His hazel eyes held wicked glints of green as he took her firmly in his arms and kissed her on the mouth. 'How wrong can a guy get? I've never wanted to kiss my sister as I've wanted to kiss you ever since you told lies about me to the police!' He was laughing, and Tricia tore herself from his embrace and ran out into the ward.

'Finished the instruments, Nurse?' asked Nurse Stephens.

'Not quite. I got held up with Dr Clancy,' she said, and wanted to giggle hysterically. I was really held up, she thought, and twitched her cap to make sure it was in place. 'I wondered if you wanted them boiled or just placed in a drum for the autoclave,' she added with sudden inspiration.

'Just boil them and put them away until we need them. We keep those handy in case of emergency dressings and we bring up the more complicated sets of instruments for taking out tubes and clips, and we always have a drum ready for serious cases like Ivor when he comes back, in case his lung collapses again. He's nearly ready to return. They took out a nasty splinter of bone embedded in one lung.'

'Poor Ivor! Does that mean he has to stay in for the other operation on his knee?'

'Oh, no! Dr Clancy did that at the same time. He went to the theatre and was going to watch Dr Boris, but everything was going so smoothly that he suggested carrying on with the knee op. Mr Attril was free and they found two teams of nurses, so they did two ops on the same man, and both were very successful. Ivor has almost forgotten he came in for that knee, and Dr Clancy's very pleased, as he did it alone, with Mr Attril standing by.'

'But Dr Clancy isn't an orthopaedic surgeon, is he?' queried Tricia.

'When he was in Accident he had to operate on whatever came in, just as they do in wartime, I believe. That programme *MASH* isn't an exaggeration. He's gaining such a variety of experience that he could do anything if called on when he goes to Canada to his sister. He even says he likes the idea of primitive facilities to see what can be done.' Nurse Stephens laughed. 'They'll probably give him a job in some really well equipped hospital in Toronto or Montreal and he'll never even see a logging camp or wherever he thinks he's going. The knee didn't take long to do, and they were free to leave while the other op, which took much longer, was finished.'

So he had time to take silly pictures but not to keep his date with Sister King, Tricia thought, and wondered just what had happened to that photograph.

She ventured back to the clinical-room, and it was empty. With a sigh, she finished her work and tidied the examination trays, noting where each one was and trying to remember all she had been taught about them, until she was sent down for a tea-break and told to bring up any X-rays and notes that might be needed from Outpatients.

She saw that two patients had walked up and were sitting in the day-room, and as she passed by the lift doors, a porter pushed a trolley out into the corridor and along to the ward. The man on the trolley looked jaundiced and very tired, as if he was glad to be lying down.

Tricia hurried through her break and ran across to her room, suddenly unsure if it could possibly be true that she had taken the snap of herself and put it somewhere before closing the folder. Dr Clancy was so certain that it wasn't with the others, she thought, but she was relieved to find no sign of it on her dressing-table.

She left her own pack and went back through Casualty to ask about the X-rays. 'There are four admissions for Ward Seven,' the staff nurse said. 'X-rays for Mr Carter, who's the jaundiced man, are here, and here are his notes. Mr Mark for a hernia op tomorrow, and Mr Browning who's been in for investigation of thyroid on Men's Medical and is now for operation after a short break at home. They both took their own notes up to the ward.'

'I saw them in the day-room,' said Tricia. 'You said four, Nurse?'

'Sister Stafford will go mad! Last year we admitted a Swede and nobody could understand him, and, more important, we couldn't tell him what we required. Have you ever tried to mime an enema? Nobody to interpret, and it took three days to find a volunteer from the Swedish Embassy to come and straighten everything out so that the poor man could have his op. After that they arranged a daily chat by phone, which seemed to work.'

'You mean we have a foreign patient again?' Tricia looked amused.

'Monsieur Bayard, from somewhere near the Camargue in France. Speaks only French and glowers at everyone. Fortunately Paul Jeffrey can talk to him in French, but he can't be in two places at once and Cas is busy just now.' Staff Nurse grinned. 'Like to take him with you? The porters are all busy and he needs a cup of tea or something to make him smile just once! I think he can go in a chair as he refuses to lie down, but be careful, as he's probably a sub-acute appendix. On second thoughts, don't give him tea as he might have to go to Theatre tonight.'

'Right!' Tricia took a deep breath and wondered if she had forgotten all her French. She went up to the dark-skinned man, who glared at her as if she might pounce on him with a scalpel. 'Ça va, Monsieur Bayard?' she said.

A torrent of fast French assailed her ears and she held up a hand and smiled, then asked him to speak slowly so that she could understand. A hesitant conversation gained courage as they went up in the lift, and he relaxed. He told her he had come off a ship in London Docks and had been brought by ambulance to the Princess Beatrice Hospital where nobody understood him and he had a pain, a bad pain that the blond doctor had said must have attention, under the knife.

'I understand,' Tricia assured him, and when she handed him over to Sister Stafford he was calmer and less aggressive.

'French? That's all we need!' groaned Sister. 'I never could do languages, and I'm not starting now! Does he really understand you, Nurse? Well, that's a relief, and I expect some of the other nurses can speak enough French to be understood.'

'*Non! Non!*' Monsieur Bayard shouted when Tricia walked away.

'Oh, dear, he's going to be difficult,' sighed Sister. 'Right, Nurse, as he seems to trust you, get him undressed and ready for examination. Explain that he mustn't drink or eat and we shall paint his tummy a pretty shade of orange before he goes down to the theatre.'

Tricia raised her eyebrows. 'I'll do my best, Sister. What's the French for orange paint?'

'Use your initiative, Nurse Metcalf,' Sister said airily, and left her alone with the patient behind the closed curtains.

Once he was settled comfortably, Tricia told Monsieur Bayard that she must leave him to see to her other work on the ward, but if he wanted anything, to ask anyone who passed by the bed for Nurse Metcalf. 'Try to rest, and the doctor will be here soon to tell you what's going to be done.'

'Leave the curtains, Nurse,' said Sister. 'Nurse Stephens is bringing the preparation trolley and Monsieur Bayard will go down to Theatre in about an hour. Dr Clancy is on his way to examine his chest and he'll be giving the anaesthetic. Just explain, will you?'

'But, Sister, I'm supposed to be doing lockers and tidying beds before any visitors come in.'

'Stay with him, Nurse. You've obviously put him at ease, and Nurse Allen can do your work.' Sister smiled and took the man's wrist in her hand. 'Yes, stay with him until he's had his pre-med after Dr Clancy leaves. His pulse is rapid, as we expect with an acute appendix, but with greater volume now, and his breathing is less fraught than when you brought him to the ward. He's relaxed and he might even begin to like it here!'

She smiled at the surprised look on Tricia's face. 'In time, Nurse, you too will be able to assess a patient even from a distance, noting how he looks, the facial colour and tension and the respiration rate. All very important even before a formal examination, as the patient is unaware of being observed so he breathes as normally as he can. You know how conscious you can become about your own respiration when you actively think about breathing. It comes in irregular bursts, not softly and silently with a good rhythm as it would do if you weren't concentrating on it.'

'I'll do my best, but I doubt if I know all the French for the medical terms, Sister,' Tricia told her.

'He seems to understand you, so do your best. Maybe Dr Clancy speaks French,' was all the help Sister gave her junior nurse. 'Tell him you'll go down to Theatre with him. You can stay until he's anaesthetised. That should please him.' She laughed, and left Tricia to struggle through the explanations. What's anaesthetic in French? she wondered.

Staff Nurse Dahlia Stephens peeped round the edge of the curtain. 'Dr Clancy is coming now,' she said. 'I'll bring the trolley and do the prep after he's gone. Does he know what's happening?'

'I think so,' Tricia said doubtfully. 'At least he

knows that a doctor is coming to see him and that he'll have to go down to an operating theatre.'

'Fill in his admission form, Nurse. We must know the address of next of kin and the usual things, and the girl who does admissions speaks no French.'

'Help!' groaned Tricia. 'How can I ask about childhood diseases? What's chickenpox and mumps in French?'

'Ask what he had as a child and write it in French. That lazy cow who swans around with a clipboard all day can get a dictionary!'

'Who's a lazy cow?' grinned Dr Clancy. 'Really, Dahlia, I had no idea there was anyone in the whole world you disliked.'

'Not you, anyway. You're a good worker, Dr Clancy, and poor little Nurse here is a bit over-worked. I'll be back with the trolley in ten minutes, if that gives you time to examine Monsieur Bayard,' said Nurse Stephens.

'*Comment allez-vous*?' Dr Clancy asked, with great assurance.

'*Ah, vous comprenez français, Monsieur le docteur*?'

'Er—not really.'

Tricia stifled a giggle. It was wonderful to see the sudden deflation of the doctor who had taken it for granted that he could insult her, treat her like a little pet, and then kiss her as if he had every right to do so. 'I've told him what to expect,' she ventured demurely, and unbuttoned the patient's pyjama jacket so that the doctor could go over his chest. She

held Monsieur Bayard forward and the chest examination was complete.

'Fine. *Très bien*,' the doctor said awkwardly, and
gently palpated the tense abdomen. 'Has he eaten
anything lately?'

'Nothing for at least five hours, and then it was
only a drink.'

'Is the pain worse today? He seems very tender all
over his abdomen and not just in the right iliac fossa
where the pain is usually felt in cases such as this.'

'All over, he told me, but not worse,' Tricia told
him.

'Right. I'm just going to take a blood sample in
case we have to cross-match and tranfuse him. We
ought to have a specimen of urine too. He came to
the ward so fast that there hasn't been time for the
routine things.'

Tricia's eyes widened. 'How do I ask him that?'

Dr Clancy grinned, obviously glad she didn't know
it all. 'Strike a bargain,' he said. 'You go and get a
urinal, then leave me to get the specimen while you
find a syringe and swabs and two specimen jars, one
for urine, one for blood.'

'Thank you.' She almost ran to find Dahlia
Stephens to ask for a syringe, then took a urinal
covered with a white cloth in to the doctor. 'I need
two jars. Dr Clancy is getting his specimen,' she told
the staff nurse when she collected the syringe. 'His
French is worse than Sister's.'

'My, oh, my, and aren't you delighted to be one
up on the handsome doctor!' Dahlia laughed. 'He's
everyone's golden boy who's nice to us all and never

singles anyone out as special, which makes a lot of girls real mad.'

'*I'm* not bothered,' said Tricia, and took the dish with the syringe back to the cubicle, followed by Dahlia's derisive laughter.

CHAPTER FOUR

'YOU'D better have supper before Mr Bayard comes back, Nurse Metcalf,' Sister said. 'I want you here to speak to him when he wakes. We're getting busy and Ivor is being transferred to us again as they need his bed in Recovery. The accident cases are really bad, and one is on a life support machine, which means that Intensive Care can't keep anyone longer than necessary.'

She looked up from the notes on the desk. 'When you come back, give Mr Carter one last drink of glucose and orange, then take away the water jug and glasses from his locker as he'll be given a sedative and nothing further by mouth so that he's ready for the theatre tomorrow. We have quite a list. Mr Carter's to have a cholecystectomy, to remove his gallbladder. His frequent attacks of pain each time gallstones lodged in the bile duct have weakened him, and from the jaundice it's obvious that he has a stone wedged there now, preventing the bile from escaping to the intestine.'

'He looks ill, Sister,' Tricia commented.

'It's an acute condition, but they may be able to do a much less traumatic operation than was usual a few years ago. It's possible to make a small incision and follow X-ray pictures to direct the surgeon to the affected part with optic fibre illumination, so

70

that the stone or the gallbladder can be removed safely and quickly with little after-care required. It means the patient goes home quickly with no complications if he's lucky! But the poor anaesthetist must be ready to keep him asleep for much longer if the surgeon can't use that approach and has to make a deeper incision with much more surgical shock.'

'And the others, Sister?'

'I'm glad you show an interest, Nurse, but you must go to supper now and I'll try to give you a report before you go off duty. I must finish my report book and be ready for Ivor's return. He's recovering nicely, but is still on a four-hourly respiration chart.'

Tricia smiled. Sister Stafford was once more in her element, with her mind full of her work and mentally ready with sleeves rolled up for whatever came her way. 'Take your full half-hour and have a good meal, as I might want you to stay on after the night staff are here, to be with Mr Bayard until he understands again where he is and what's been done.'

'Yes, Sister.' Tricia walked lightly down the corridor, feeling important for the first time since she had joined Men's Surgical. She also felt very sorry for Monsieur Bayard, alone in a foreign country where he had never really met the people, except in docks where his merchant ship berthed, and then only in passing. She went to her room and found an old English-French dictionary, which she took with her to supper and sat over her lamb chops and mashed potatoes and beans, looking up words and phrases to freshen her memory, but there were few medical terms and she was really no wiser after studying the book than she had been earlier.

The evening was warm and the sky dressed with puffs of white cloud edged with pink and turquoise. She paused to watch a dense mass of starlings weave against the sky, seem to hang for a moment, motionless, then turn together to roost high in the towers of the ruined oratory in the park and under the old railway bridge, and as always when faced with something beautiful, she felt sad, as if something was lacking, some person who should share the moment and the feeling with her was not there, and yet she had nobody who would fit into her dream.

Reluctantly, she walked back on duty. What a picture that would have made, she thought, but she knew she needed faster film and better equipment to take such pictures. A camera like Dr Clancy had in the park, maybe, and she recalled the high quality of his photographs.

She heard lift doors slam and hurried to the ward. Monsieur Bayard had been lifted on to the bed and a nasal-stomach tube was being strapped to his cheek. Dr Clancy, in a plastic theatre apron and a disposable cap, stood by the bed taking the patient's blood pressure, and Sister patted the pale cheek gently to make the patient respond and come awake.

'He should respond now, Sister. I kept him as light as possible with curare and the minimum of gases, but from the colour of his fingers you can tell he's a heavy smoker and we must be careful to avoid chest complications, so Physio must be told to get him breathing as quickly as possible. French-speaking, if possible!' Dr Clancy saw that Tricia was hovering uncertainly and grinned. 'Over to you, Nurse Metcalf. Talk to him and make him answer you. He must regain consciousness before we allow him to sleep naturally. Sounds crazy, but that's how the body works.'

'What do I say?' Tricia queried.

'Ask him how he feels and then ask the name of his wife or mother or whoever's the next of kin. Tell him he's been a good patient, or tell him you love him, but say something!'

'We have the names of next of kin on the notes. He told me all that earlier,' she said.

'You know that, and I know that, but we want to know he understands what we're saying, however imperfect our French! I'll be back later.'

He left in a hurry to give an anaesthetic to one of the building site accident cases in Orthopaedics, and Tricia stood by the bed making remarks in French until Monsieur Bayard opened his eyes and saw her. He half smiled, answered all her questions intelligently and drifted off into natural sleep.

'Good,' said Sister. 'Stay with him, Nurse, until the night staff take over. He might wake up in pain and you'll be useful to let him know what they did to him.'

'What did they do, Sister?' Tricia asked.

'The appendix was perforated and a drain was necessary, although they seldom use one now as they usually catch the appendix in time, but he has a corrugated drain, which will make his dressing very messy. Night staff will pack his dressing later and re-do the whole thing before we come back on duty tomorrow. He must keep his hands away from the dressing.'

'How do I say all that?' Tricia wondered aloud when Sister had gone.

'All what?' Paul Jeffrey lounged by the bed, regarding her with considerable interest. 'You look better out of uniform,' he remarked, 'but still very tasty.'

'I speak a little French, but I can't think how to tell Monsieur Bayard that he has a drain in his wound and that he must keep his hands away from it,' she replied, ignoring the familiar tone that the casualty officer adopted.

'He's stirring. Shall I have a go?'

'Could you?' she said gratefully. 'I'd hate to tell him the wrong thing.'

'That would never do. We don't want to tell him he has a large industrial sewer in his side instead of a simple drain, do we?' Paul Jeffrey sounded mocking, but Tricia was alarmed, and confessed that she had no idea of what to tell him. Paul laughed. 'Very well, I'll tell him—but remember, you'll owe me for this.'

Monsieur Bayard groaned and his hand moved under the bedclothes towards the dressing. Tricia called him by name and he opened his eyes slightly. 'Monsieur Bayard,' she repeated, and his gaze focused on her.

'*Ecoutez*!' Paul Jeffrey said sharply, and a flood of very fluent French followed, leaving Monsieur

Bayard in no doubt about what had been done, his present condition and the fact that if he pulled out the drain, then he personally, the casualty officer of the Princess Beatrice Hospital, would take him back to the operating theatre to put it in again!

'You've frightened him,' Tricia said reproachfully.

'At least he knows the score,' Paul said calmly. 'Better to be a bit hard to get the message across and let it stick. What treatment is planned? Once he knows, he won't need you until tomorrow and I can walk you home. I'll come up early to see he behaves.'

'He'll be having the dressing packed later and a full dressing tomorrow,' she said. 'Oh, Sister said he must remember to take deep breaths, and the physio people will see him tomorrow.' Paul nodded and explained to the patient, then told him to get to sleep.

'I also said he might need something for pain later and a nurse would come and give him an injection,' he added.

'Thank you. I was so worried that I'd say the wrong thing,' Tricia confessed.

'Now say the right thing. Say, Thank you, Paul, and yes, I'd love to have dinner with you on my next evening off.'

'I. . .don't know when that will be,' she said, wondering how she could refuse.

'Ask Sister in the morning,' he said. 'You must have a rota of sorts. On this evening, so off tomorrow?'

'But you don't know me,' she protested.

'Better than you think. After all, I have your picture next to my heart.'

'You haven't!' Tricia exclaimed, and stared as he waved a photograph under her nose. 'Where did you get that?'

The picture had been torn across and put together again with sticky transparent tape and was slightly crumpled as if it had been torn and then thrown away in a waste basket, but she recognised the print that Dr Clancy had taken of her in the park. Behind her the luxuriant foliage and deeply coloured flowers bloomed, with touches of pale blue evening sky behind the setting, and she noticed that her thin baggy cotton top of deep sludgy green was pulled across her breasts in the breeze, outlining her figure sweetly and giving her the appearance of a dryad of the woods.

'I saw it being mutilated and wondered what could have caused so much annoyance on the face of our lovely casualty sister, so when she left the office I slipped in and found this in the waste basket.' He held out his hand for the photograph. 'Finders keepers,' he said calmly, and took it from her nerveless fingers. 'But I'm puzzled to know why she had it in the first place. It's a good picture, and when you get more prints taken off, please, pretty please, I'd like one without sticky tape. It does nothing for you, but the best I could do as an emergency repair.'

'I didn't take it,' she began, and he laughed.

'Of course you didn't take your own picture. You had an accomplice who did rather well.'

'It wasn't my camera or my film, and I had no idea

it was being taken,' she said, wondering how she could keep Dr Clancy out of the conversation.

'Then who at Beattie's has a good camera and likes taking pictures of trees and usually the more mundane things, but who might just be stirred to take a picture of a pretty girl?' His eyes mocked her but had become hard. 'Surely Ruth's dear Matthew Clancy wouldn't give her a photograph of another woman? That would really bring down the wrath of hell on his head!'

'He didn't——' Tricia began, but heard footsteps and a night nurse came into the cubicle.

'Thanks a lot, Metcalf,' she said. 'The SNO on night duty asked me to take over and do this hourly chart. I speak French, so you can go off now, but I know how important your contribution has been,' she added kindly, taking it for granted that the tension in the girl's face was due to the strain of talking to a foreign patient when she had little nursing experience and only a superficial knowledge of his language.

'Dr Jeffrey's French was better,' Tricia admitted with a forced smile, and he bowed slightly, smiling.

'That's nice. Dulwich, isn't it? I keep meaning to go and see the flowers, but each year I miss them,' said Nurse Thomas. 'Part-time night duty and two kids at home make me knackered and I just put my feet up and watch telly, so tonight will be a rest if I special Monsieur Bayard.' She held the photograph and examined it again. 'My eldest has a nice camera. Maybe he ought to go to the park. I'd like a picture of the rhododendrons.' She smiled at Paul Jeffrey. 'You take a good snap. Pity it got torn.'

'I think that's mine.' A hand snaked across Nurse Thomas's shoulder and took the print. 'I've been looking for it everywhere,' said Dr Clancy. 'You can go now, Jeffrey,' he added curtly, for once pulling rank, but ignoring Tricia completely. 'Nurse Thomas speaks French well and you have no patients on this ward, have you? There's no reason for you to stay.'

Monsieur Bayard groaned and Nurse Thomas went to the bedside, talking softly. 'He needs an injection, Doctor,' she said.

Matthew Clancy put the photograph away in an inside pocket and took out a pen. 'I came to write up for morphine for the first injection, a smaller one in four hours' time and then for any other milder drugs he may need. He must also have a full course of antibiotics as his appendix was a mess, and later we must make sure his blood count is OK.'

He turned the limp arm over and pointed out three needle marks that he'd seen in the theatre when he had given intravenous Thiopentone to begin the anaesthetic. 'Later, Nurse, I'd like you to ask him what he had before he came in here. There aren't enough marks to indicate permanent drug abuse, but maybe the ship's doctor gave him something when they were at sea and they couldn't operate.' He sighed. 'No notes came with him, so even giving him an antibiotic has its dangers. We don't know if he's allergic to penicillin, and he may have been dosed up with any of several things on the ship, and formed a resistance to whatever it was if taken over a fairly long period.'

Tricia watched him write, and backed away, hoping to escape but disliking the idea of leaving with Paul Jeffrey, who tried to take her arm to get her out of the ward. A wave of depression engulfed her. Everything she did was wrong in the eyes of the man who had become ridiculously important to her. She wanted to tell him he had a completely wrong idea about her, but what could she say?

As if aware of her presence, Matthew Clancy said without looking away from the patient, 'Nurse Metcalf, I'd be obliged if you'd wait. I want to talk to you.'

Paul Jeffrey shrugged and slipped away, looking annoyed, but whispered, 'We have a date tomorrow, remember. Pick you up at seven.'

'No!' she said clearly, and Nurse Thomas looked surprised and a bit shocked as she thought that this very junior nurse was refusing to obey a senior doctor.

'Dr Clancy is nearly through,' she said. 'I know you're off duty late, but surely you can wait for five more minutes?'

'I wasn't talking about that,' Tricia said unhappily.

Nurse Thomas raised her eyebrows, not having seen Paul Jeffrey leave or heard him speak. 'Well, you know what they say if you start talking to yourself!' she said.

'There,' said Dr Clancy. 'I've written him up for Erythromycin which is similar to penicillin but safer if he's penicillin-resistant and it works on intestinal

conditions as well as a lot of other conditions. I'd
like to give him a much stronger drug, but I think
we'd better be conservative until he can tell us what
he's had in the past. He may not even know the
names, but we shall hear the usual answer but in
French this time: "Well, Doctor, I had some pink
pills or green pills or little white pills!" which isn't a
lot of help.' He handed the chart to Nurse Thomas.
'Bring the first morphine injection and give it while
we're here so he isn't left alone,' he suggested, and
she hurried away and came back with the syringe
and phial, ready to have the dose checked as it was
on the dangerous drugs list.

Tricia took the dish to the clinical-room, where
the disposable syringe was broken before being
discarded in the garbage, to prevent it being taken
away and used again, while Nurse Thomas locked
the phial of morphine sulphate away in the inner
compartment of the drug cupboard. Maybe now I
can slip away and he'll have forgotten that he wanted
to see me, Tricia thought hopefully, but Dr Clancy
had discarded his plastic apron and cap, which he
left on the floor of the room for Nurse Thomas to
pick up and send back to the theatre on the trolley
when it was collected, and was leaning against the
wall in the corridor.

'Your place or mine?' he said, and smiled at the
startled glance the young nurse gave him. 'Don't
worry—I just want a chat over a cup of coffee. I had
no supper and I need coffee and biscuits, that is if
you aren't efficient enough to serve me a four-course
dinner?'

'As your sisters would do if you looked ever so slightly hungry?' she asked to hide her nervousness.

'Actually no. They're great, but none of them can cook well. Much too keen on being career women, and when I go home they treat me abominably.' He tried to look pathetic but failed.

'Plenty of coffee in Casualty,' she suggested. 'But Sister King is off duty now, so it might be cold.'

'We can get some in the cafeteria next to Casualty,' he said. 'Paper cups, but the best I can think of at this hour.' Tricia thought of the rather bleak room where relatives of patients could wait for news and have coffee and sandwiches and biscuits, and staff on duty late or called up in an emergency were often glad to have a hot drink. She also recalled how nurses in uniform were often asked questions about patients who were nothing to do with the wards on which they worked, which was embarrassing, so they had no privacy over a welcome cup of coffee.

'I could make some coffee and at least I can offer a china mug,' she said. 'We can have it in the sitting-room of the staff hostel,' she added hastily, in case he had any ideas of going to her room.

'Fine.' He gathered up his briefcase and jacket and swung beside her along the corridor in silence. Tricia glanced at his set face and her heart sank. It was as bad as waiting for a telling-off by one of the senior nursing officers, when she was in preliminary training school and spilled the water used to bed-bath that awful plastic dummy they used for practice.

'Lovely evening,' she tried to say, but no sound

came, but Dr Clancy seemed to share her idea, for he paused in the doorway leading to the main drive and took a deep breath of fresh air. The dusk had deepened into a pearly after-glow, with the red haze of distant London traffic away across the city and a flittering of bats venturing out of the park to hunt. 'I hate bats,' she said.

'Why? It's fashionable to like them, droppings and all,' he said, and she saw the glint of white teeth as he smiled. 'Afraid they'll nest in your hair?' He brushed back his own tawny mane and laughed. 'I'm taller than you and have much more foliage, so they'll get me first.'

'These aren't so bad, although I hate anything that's silent and swift, but when we were in Africa I saw huge ones that terrified me, even though they didn't come close.' She shivered and he put a comforting arm round her shoulder.

'Harmless fruit bats,' he said. 'You should have taken a picture of them and really looked at them closely. They say phobias disappear if you're brave enough to face them, just as in *The Pilgrim's Progress*, the lions got smaller and smaller as Christian approached them and were harmless as he passed them, instead of devouring him as he expected.'

They had reached the hostel and found the sitting-room empty. Quickly Tricia went into the kitchen and put ground coffee into the percolator from her own labelled tin which she had hidden on the top of the row of cupboards. She dashed up to her room and brought back an unopened tin of biscuits that an aunt had given her the last time she was in London as a gift from Belgium, and Matthew Clancy eyed it with interest.

'Could you open the seal while I get the coffee?' she asked, and came back with coffee, sugar and a jar of coffee whitener. 'Sorry, no cream,' she said. She regarded him with amusement mixed with faint irritation. He sat back in a comfortable chair with the open biscuit tin in his lap, selecting all the chocolate ones.

'I'm glad you like *my* biscuits,' she said sarcastically. 'Coffee? Let me take that tin from you to give you a free hand.' Deliberately she removed all the rest of the chocolate biscuits from the top layer and put them on her plate.

'Hey, you've swiped the lot!' he complained in an aggrieved tone. 'You've had supper.'

'Do your sisters ever see a chocolate biscuit when you're around?' she asked sweetly.

'Never,' he assured her. 'I try to keep them slim.'

'So I'm not entirely like your sisters,' she said, and lowered her eyelids to hide the smile that refused to go away. She forgot that he had made her have coffee with him as if he had something to say to her that she wouldn't like hearing, and she began to enjoy his company. This lion had not grown smaller as she approached him and she still felt cautious in his company, but on closer inspection he hadn't become large and frightening either. His voice was deep and attractive, his body relaxed and very masculine as he reclined in the deep chair and looked at her with a half smile that was the only thing that made her feel uneasy.

'No, you're not like any of my sisters tonight,' he said. 'They'd let me look at the next layer of biscuits and then I could take what I wanted and replace them with the ones I don't like from the top layer.'

'Do you always do that?' Tricia pretended to be shocked.

'What? Eat all the best biscuits or take what I want from life?'

Her eyelids fluttered and she moved restlessly, but made no answer. His eyes were more green tonight and she saw that his expression had changed. Her heart beat fast as he left the chair and sat on the edge of the settee next to her. Tricia sipped at an empty mug and he took it away from her. He was so close that his breath on her cheek was soft and intimate. She closed her eyes.

'More coffee?' he asked, and took both the mugs to the table to fill again, and in passing sneaked a chocolate biscuit from her uneaten share.

'Be my guest,' she said faintly, and felt an acute sense of anticlimax. No wonder Sister King got mad when he was so casual! Any woman would be driven up the wall by such a man, she decided, and tried to forget his hands, so gentle on a patient's painful body, so expert in his work; and his eyes that promised deep emotion but withheld exactly what he was thinking.

He brought the coffee and sat beside her. 'I do take some things I want, like photographs,' he said as if he was now fed and able to cope with unpleasant facts. 'Once I've taken them they're mine. Even if pictures are used to illustrate books they remain the copyright of the photographer and not the subject, so the pictures we had developed last week are mine and nobody had the right to take one and keep it, or worse still, attempt to destroy it.'

'I can't imagine what happened,' she replied firmly. 'I did see the snap, but it was in the folder when I left it with Sister King to give to you.'

'That was in her office?'

'That's right. She said she'd be seeing you and would make sure you had the pictures.'

'You examined them first?' His voice was cool.

'The girl in the chemist's shop asked me to see that they were the right ones, and I glanced at them to see if I could find a familiar scene or someone in them that I recognised,' she explained.

'And, surprise! There you were, taken unawares?'

'Yes.'

'So you took another peep in Ruth's office and decided that I'd been a bit presumptuous and tore it in half and tossed it in the waste bin?'

'No!' she said, her eyes wide and very blue.

'And then Paul Jeffrey came in and saw what you'd done and asked if he could have it?' His mouth tightened. 'Who supplied the sticky tape? It must have been a bit of a giggle. Were you flattered that Paul wanted it so badly? He's had plenty of practice and most girls are a pushover for him. Be warned, Trixie.'

'What an absurd idea. . .and I'm not your sister Trixie who can be bullied by her great big brother!'

He sighed, as if he was very disappointed. 'It's no use. Ruth told me what happened when I asked if she'd seen the snap, as it was missing. She walked in on you two, and admitted that she felt cross that a junior nurse could take such liberties on duty. To give her due respect, she didn't want to say anything about it.'

'But she managed to do so! If that's what you think, then I can't help it. Believe her, for all I care.'

'I've known Ruth for years, or Trixie has, and I've met her many times. She has no reason to lie about such a trivial matter.'

'Trivial?' she echoed. 'You make it seem a capital offence! Ask Paul what really happened, if you want the truth.'

'The truth, from Jeffrey?' He gave a short laugh.

'Does it really matter? I know it had nothing to do with me and so does he.' Tricia's lips trembled. 'Why do men want a kind of trophy to make them feel they almost own a person's soul?' She thought back to the man in the Navy who had wanted her as a casual lover and took her picture to add to his gallery of conquests.

History was repeating itself, she thought bitterly. Paul had taken away a snap, that to be honest he had a right to take as it had been thrown away, and now Matthew Clancy looked anything but the relaxed and sweet man everyone told her he was. Tears clouded her eyes as she felt strong fingers digging into the soft flesh of her shoulders. Matthew shook her and his voice was husky. 'You little fool, can't you see that the photograph means nothing? I can get a hundred taken off if I want them, or have one blown up life-size to stick on the wall!'

'Then why the fuss?' she breathed.

'It was mine, and you tore it up and gave it to Jeffrey, of all people,' he said, and there was desolation in his voice. 'Why him?' He held her roughly and kissed her lips with such force that she felt the impact of his teeth on her lips, in a union of raw passion but no gentle desire; a kiss born of frustrated pride and simple male arrogance, and the suspicion that another man had something that he just might want some time in the future or whenever it suited him to pick the fruit.

Tricia tore away from him and sobbed, 'I'm glad he took the picture and kept it. At least he hasn't forced me to kiss him like that, and he treats me as if he really likes me!'

Matthew stared at her as if recovering from a trance, and she dashed away the tears and dried her eyes. She slammed down the lid on the biscuit tin as if that was very important and put the empty mugs on the tray.

'Oh, good, someone's made coffee. Is there any left? I slipped over for something from my room and couldn't face the sludge left in the dining-room.' The night nurse from Gynae looked at the strained faces and wondered what was going on between the best-looking man at Beattie's and the rather small first-year student nurse. Tricia heated up the rest of the coffee and fetched a mug. 'Thanks, dear. Saved my life,' said Nurse Miller. She glanced at her watch. 'I've got ten minutes,' she said comfortably. 'Tell me all the news. I've had nights off and missed the panic over Rose Day. What exactly happened?'

'Have a biscuit,' Matthew offered. 'You don't mind, do you, Nurse?' he asked politely. 'There are some rather nice chocolate biscuits left, that Nurse Metcalf forgot to put back in the tin when we'd finished our snack.'

'Were you off late?' Nurse Miller asked.

'Very late, and starving as I missed supper,' he replied easily. 'Nurse Metcalf had a very trying evening too, as she had to cope with a language difficulty in Ward Seven and a general breakdown of communication that was most regrettable,' he added with a glance at Tricia's set face. There was pleading in his eyes, but she ignored it, remembering only the onslaught of wounded masculinity that had shown that he wanted her but had no real deep tender feeling for her. A spoiled child who reached out for what he wanted and hated being frustrated. And tomorrow he'll want another toy, she decided, and hardened her heart even though her whole body was limp with the memory of his arms about her.

Sister Ruth King almost threw herself at him whenever he appeared, and he accepted it as his due, but he didn't seem all that attracted to her. Maybe that was what all men were like, she thought. The thrill of the chase was all-important and they tired of easy quarries. If I'd tried to attract him maybe he wouldn't have bothered to kiss me like that but would have believed he had plenty of time to move in if he felt the inclination. If I'm nice to Paul Jeffrey when he takes me out to dinner, then

maybe he too will have no urgent desire to chase me
seriously! I shall go out with him, she decided. Why
not? Matthew Clancy is far too senior a man, far too
experienced and far too attractive to bother with me
except as a joke.

'So there was a man who tried to abduct nurses?'
Nurse Miller sipped her coffee and listened avidly.

'Yes, we had to fetch the nurses selling roses much
earlier than planned as two nurses had been badly
frightened,' Matthew Clancy told her. He glanced at
Tricia, as if he wanted to forget what had happened
and to put matters on a safer level between them,
but Nurse Miller was determined to stay for as long
as possible and Tricia was gathering up her belongings to go to her room. 'Don't take the biscuits away
yet, Nurse Miller's still hungry,' he said in a vain
attempt to keep Tricia there.

'I've had enough, thank you. What an unexpected
treat! Get to bed, Nurse. You look very tired. Do
you find Men's Surgical more trying than Gynae? I
remember you there before you went into Block for
lectures.'

'I do find men much more difficult,' Tricia admitted. 'I think women on the whole are far nicer.' She
gave a half smile. 'Some men get very odd ideas and
some really are the pits!'

'Better tell the medical staff to watch it, Dr
Clancy,' Nurse Miller warned. 'It sounds as if we
have a man-hater at Beattie's!' she laughed. 'You
weren't one of the nurses accosted in the West End,
were you?'

'Actually, both Nurse Allen and I were asked for

dates by men who hung about for ages, so we said we'd meet them outside the British Museum at nine-thirty, just to get rid of them. I wonder if they all met and compared notes?' Tricia smiled. 'That wasn't threatening as they all seemed quite normal, it was daylight in a busy place and they weren't in cars, so we felt safe, especially as a very nice policeman kept an eye on us, but the other man was different, I believe.'

'Did they get a good description of him?' Nurse Miller looked fascinated.

'I think they did, but of course there may have been more than one,' said Tricia. A smile that was full of malice made her face light up. 'Our very nice policeman took one description of a man with ginger hair wearing a tracksuit.'

Dr Clancy coughed and went red. 'That's the one, I'll bet,' Nurse Miller said with conviction.

'I'm going to bed,' said Tricia. 'I'm sure Dr Clancy will escort you back to the hospital, Nurse Miller. He'll protect you from the bats as everyone says he wouldn't hurt a fly.'

CHAPTER FIVE

'GO DOWN and wait by the theatre door until the porter brings Mr Mark out on the trolley, Nurse Metcalf. Should be straightforward. No drip and they haven't taken long over the op, so I must make sure Mr Carter is ready to be taken down when they're ready for him.' Sister Stafford glanced at the neatly made post-operative bed behind the half-closed curtains and smiled. 'Even Nurse Allen should be satisfied we aren't wasting her talents today! With five operations she's been really busy, getting the beds ready.'

'Is Mr Carter the last case, Sister?'

'Yes—as you know, we do all the clean surgery first, like hernias and thyroids, to avoid cross-infection. After last night they had to clean the theatre extra thoroughly and disinfect everything in sight ready for today, after Monsieur Bayard spilled potential infection from his burst appendix. Mr Carter is our last case and possibly he has an infection as well as stones in the gallbladder, so that's why he's last on the list. You noticed that we put him on intravenous saline and glucose to get some fluid into him while he was allowed nothing by mouth before the operation, and he'll have a drip for quite a while, so handle the tube and bag carefully, Nurse.'

Tricia hurried down the corridor and ran down the stairs rather than wait for the lift. The well-polished floor led to the quiet sterility of the theatre annexe and the faint smell of antiseptics and ether filtered out from the anaesthetic-room. Through the round port-hole window in the main door she peeped at masked figures, gowned in green with theatre caps tied firmly across brows that could have been male or female from that distance. Nurses in white gowns moved swiftly to clear swabs from the counting rack, to put back the gown in which the patient had arrived for his operation and to help lift him carefully on to the trolley.

The doors were flung back and the trolley was pushed out by the porter and by a tall figure in theatre boots that looked enormous but only just fitted. Dr Clancy made a note on the chart and handed it to Tricia. His eyes above the mask took on the green of the theatre cotton, but she couldn't assess what thoughts went on behind the sombre stare, and as she looked at him, his glance rested on her face for a second, then flickered away as if he saw only a nurse, just any nurse about to collect a patient. 'Which end shall I take?' she asked the porter, and Dr Clancy returned to the anaesthetic-room without a backward glance at her.

'They want the next one quickly,' the porter told her. 'Mr Masters wants to get away before two o'clock. The thyroid took longer than usual and the extra hernia they slipped in from Men's Medical didn't help. Nasty cough he had,' he added cheerfully. 'Hope he doesn't bust his stitches.'

'They cancelled one op on Gynae last month because the woman had a cold,' Tricia said. 'I thought they liked to clear up anything like coughs and colds before they have anaesthetics.'

'Depends,' said the porter with an air of being in the confidence of the surgeon. 'If this one we had earlier had a heart condition or asthma, his cough might have given him the hernia in the first place, and if that strangulated during a fit of coughing then Gawd 'elp him, I say.' Tricia looked impressed until he explained, 'My brother had that, so I know all about it.'

During the next hour there was no time to think about her own troubles as the ward was frantically busy. Monsieur Bayard kept asking for her to talk to him, until Sister stood by and made her say he had to sleep and not call out every five minutes. 'Come round with me, Nurse,' ordered Sister. 'I want you to take each pulse after I do and write down what it is on this chart paper, count the respirations and put that figure in another column, and later I shall compare your figures with mine to find out how accurate you are.'

Tricia followed her to the first bed, which the earliest case of the day, Mr Browning, who had now lost seven-eighths of his thyroid gland, seemed fairly relaxed and lay half asleep, lying on his back. He was allowed one pillow. Sister took a pretty little gold watch from her breast pocket where it was pinned and smiled. 'You're doing very well, Mr Browning,' she told him. 'Nurse and I are going to check your pulse, then I think you can have more pillows.' She looked at the notes from the theatre. 'They found that the thyroid was very big and you may find that your voice is husky or difficult for a while, but that does happen after this operation and means that the gland pressed on your voice box and it might have been bruised slightly when the gland was removed. We'll come back and make you comfortable, with extra pillows, after my round,' she promised him.

She felt for his pulse and timed it for a full minute, then nodded to Tricia to do the same. The pulse was rapid and—what was the word that Sister Tutor used? Thready? It was also slightly irregular, so Tricia added that to her note and carefully added the time the pulse was taken and the name of the patient before making out a fresh section for the next case.

'A finger on the pulse is still more revealing than a glance at a monitor screen,' Sister explained. 'What did you notice, Nurse?'

Tricia told her, and added, 'I see now why you took it for a full minute, Sister, instead of a quarter or half and doubling it or multiplying by four to be quicker. I didn't notice the irregular beat until nearly three-quarters of a minute had gone.'

'Good! You're beginning to think well, Nurse. Thyroids are tricky, both from the medical point of view and from our side too. Now we have to check his progress carefully, as the over-active gland has put considerable strain on his heart, hence the irregular beat, which incidentally is much better today, even such a short time after the operation. If they remove too much of the gland then they may have to give the patient extra hormones to make up, but Mr Masters is a very great surgeon who has more than skill. He has a flair for what's right and seldom makes a mistake. With all their knowledge and new discoveries, some men and women never achieve that and remain just good general surgeons.'

They went to each of the post-operative cases, and Tricia was amazed at the difference between the results. In class, they had taken each other's pulses and respirations, but with twelve healthy girls there was little of interest to show on their charts, and in the wards where she had worked to begin her training junior nurses were just that, queens of the sluice and bedpan, and never got closer than bed-making and food.

Mr Browning was smiling when they came back to him. 'Glad you told me about my voice,' he croaked. 'It doesn't hurt, but it will keep me quiet for a bit. At least my wife will get a word in edgeways now!'

'We want you to sit up straight now, Mr Browning,' Sister said. 'Together, Nurse. Lift him forward and hold him while I do the pillows.' She took the pillows one at a time from the chair where they were piled ready, and made a nest for his back and two higher rests for his head so that he was cradled in comfort but remained sitting tall, his neck swathed in bandages and his silvered hair making him look vaguely like a vicar. 'Now rest, ask for a painkiller if you need it, and, when you remember it, wriggle your toes and move your legs a little to make sure we get the circulation going,' Sister suggested. 'You haven't been sick since you returned? No nausea?'

'I woke up feeling quite clear-headed, Sister. The man with the gas tubes did me proud. When I had my hernia done thirty years ago I was very sick after the op, but today, nothing, and I was half awake on the way back to bed.'

'We've had good anaesthetists at Beattie's for a very long time,' said Sister. 'Dr Boris is the best I know in the whole profession and Dr Clancy has learned fast from him, but he's really a surgeon, and I wish he'd stick to that.' She glanced at Tricia. 'He's another one like Mr Masters, full of instinctive good sense and a very great skilled touch that works magic.' She twitched back the curtains and left Mr Browning with a clearer view of the ward.

'I finished my chart,' said Tricia, and followed Sister Stafford into the office. 'Thank you, Sister,' she said shyly. 'I've learned such a lot this morning.'

'This chart is good, Nurse. It agrees with mine, I'm relieved to see.' Sister smiled. 'You don't look quite as startled as you did the first day on the ward! Have you lost that first fear that men are awful and you could never bed-bath one or give a man a bedpan?'

'It seems stupid even to think about that now, and most of them are very nice to the nurses. It's quite fun, but they do like to suffer a lot more than women, who I think try to hide their discomfort.'

'She is learning fast,' Sister said, and laughed. 'Hello, Dr Clancy. Nurse admits after only a short

Four free Romances and two free gifts for you

As an introduction to our Reader Service, we invite you to accept four spell-binding Mills & Boon Romances plus two gifts absolutely FREE.

Romances every month!

At the same time we'll reserve a subscription for you; which means that you could go on to receive SIX BRAND NEW ROMANCES *every month*. What's more, we'll pay for all the postage and packing, and we'll include our free Newsletter - featuring recipes, author news, horoscopes, competitions, and much more.

And, as an *extra bonus*, when you return this card we'll also send you TWO FREE GIFTS - our own cuddly Teddy Bear plus an intriguing mystery gift.

So you've nothing to lose, whatever you decide, the four free books and two free gifts will be yours to keep - so don't delay, REPLY TODAY!

FREE

time here that all men aren't bad. It took me a lot longer than that!'

'But now you couldn't work in any other ward, Sister! That means something.' Matthew Clancy regarded Tricia with detached interest. 'I thought Nurse Metcalf hated men.'

'I'm quite happy to nurse them,' she said, avoiding eye contact.

'Then I know what to do if I want your attention, Nurse. What condition is free of pain but needs lots of tender loving care?' His eyes held a caress and slightly mocking approval.

'I could never nurse anyone with a personality disorder,' she said calmly, but the thought of Matthew Clancy in bed under her care was almost too much to bear, and she hoped nobody needed to take her pulse at that moment. It was the exchange that Sister expected between the good-looking doctor and any nurse with spirit and wit enough to answer his banter, and she missed the sudden tension linking them as Tricia forced herself to meet his gaze.

'You should be here as a surgeon,' Sister Stafford said severely. 'I think you're crazy to go to Canada and leave us all—for what?' She laughed. 'I think there must be more to it than treating loggers for crush syndrome and back injuries. I think he's going to get married there and she wants him to live in Canada.' She looked pensive. 'Or of course he may be running away with a broken heart. What do you think, Nurse?'

'Do you have a heart, Dr Clancy?' Tricia asked.

'I think perhaps not,' he grinned. 'But Sister knows me well. I'm always losing something, so why not my heart? Which reminds me, did I leave my case here? I left the anaesthetic registrar in charge of Mr Carter while I found some notes I want, but I have to get back as quickly as possible. It all seems quite routine so far, but Mr Masters has had to do the conventional operation as there's something stuck high up in the duct that couldn't be removed by remote control. It just went further along the duct and he has adhesions from earlier attacks which have to be broken down. We'll bring him back in about three-quarters of an hour, Sister.'

'You left your briefcase here last night and Sister King recognised it when she came up for coffee with me this morning,' said Sister Stafford. 'She took it down for you. Bleep her and ask her to leave it in the theatre. She should be on her way to lunch. Oh, no—she'll be back. I had no idea it was so late. They do keep meals hot for surgical wards on Theatre days, but you'll have to hurry down, Nurse. Take Staff Nurse with you as the rest have been down to eat.'

She glanced at the off-duty rota. 'You're off tonight, Nurse Metcalf. Make sure you get some fresh air. It's not good to sit in your room after a hard day on the ward, and although we don't make nurses tell us where they go for their off-duty, we like to think you act sensibly and have a varied and interesting off-duty. Living in the hostel is good, but it does mean that you have no need to travel far and might get into a definitely boring routine.'

'Oh, Nurse Metcalf wanders about with a camera, taking pictures of trees,' said Dr Clancy. As if it had only just occurred to him, he added, 'I brought my camera along, Sister. Seeing the pictures that Nurse Metcalf took made me think that if I go to Canada I shall want a few souvenirs of this ward and of the people with whom I worked.'

'What a lovely idea! You must show them to me and let me have a print or two,' Sister replied with enthusiasm.

'You don't think any of your staff might object?' he asked with a grin, seeing that Tricia's colour was rising.

'Of course not! They'll love it. Take Nurse Metcalf now before she goes to lunch.'

'I'll take one of you, Sister, and then get back to the theatre. I'll leave Nurse Metcalf until later.' He grinned in a way that he must have done a hundred times when teasing his sisters. 'She looks better when she's smiling.'

Tricia walked quickly away and found Dahlia Stephens in the clinical-room, stripping a dressing trolley. 'Lunch? What a good idea. I'm starving!' Nurse Stephens washed her hands thoroughly and dried them, then tidied her uniform and pushed a strand of thick curly black hair back inside her cap. 'Monsieur Bayard had a visitor,' she said wickedly. 'A friend of yours. That Dr Jeffrey really has been a help, in spite of what everyone thinks of him most of the time.'

'He speaks very fluent French,' Tricia said lightly.

'And he seemed very interested in new nurses, or

one in particular,' Dahlia Stephens went on. 'He told me you have a date with him this evening and asked me to remind you that he'll pick you up at seven.'

'*He* says that, but I haven't said I'd go out with him,' Tricia said uneasily.

'Good food and wine and good company—what more do you want, girl?' Dahlia picked up a tray at the servery. 'I'll have salad today and keep to my diet. I do try, but I get so hungry. You needn't have much now as you'll have to make room for the goodies tonight.'

'I shall try the moussaka. It doesn't look like any Greek dish I've eaten, but the Irish stew is far too full of potato.' Tricia sighed. 'I do miss good cooking and keep meaning to do some in the hostel if I can get an evening alone in the kitchen, with few people around, but I shall want someone to help me eat it all. I make far too much.'

'Please don't stand on ceremony, Nurse! You'll find that rank disappears if staff nurses smell good food and are invited to join in.' Dahlia regarded Tricia carefully. 'Go out tonight and enjoy it, but why not invite Dr Jeffrey to a meal in the hostel? If you ask him, then he can't expect to have you for dessert this evening to repay his invitation. Just because a man buys a girl a meal, he often thinks he's bought her body as well!'

Tricia laughed, her eyes sparkling with fun. 'I can imagine his face if I asked other staff as well and he couldn't have a cosy little tête-à-tête!'

'That shows you aren't bowled over by his charm,'

Dahlia said with satisfaction. 'I'm glad, as he's a bit of a womaniser.'

'Could I really give a small party?' queried Tricia. 'I'm very junior and some might say it's a bit presumptuous, but I do have a birthday looming up.'

'I'll clear it with the Senior Nursing Officer if you like. We have had a few get-togethers in the music-room. Not a lot of people use it now that so many staff live out, and it's usually free, but parties are expensive and you can't pay for everything. Why not have a kind of American supper when everyone brings enough for one?' Dahlia suggested.

'I'd rather do it alone. It's quite easy. I shall make one huge cassoulet and a quiche and maybe a pile of samosas and buy French bread. The preparation would fill a day off and the party could be in the evening.'

'Who'll be invited?'

'That's tricky.' Tricia's face cleared. 'I know—I can invite those of my set who are off that night, and spread it around that anyone who's been on Gynae and Surgical with me is welcome to pop in for a snack.' She giggled. 'I might not need to invite Dr Jeffrey, but it would be the perfect way out if he gets too possessive. I have no need to tell him it's a party for more than two!'

'Isn't it too ambitious?' queried Dahlia.

'No. I love cooking and I have so little chance to do any. The kitchen here is wasted, as the cooker is fairly new and the fridge is big and there are pots that haven't seen the light of day but could be fine after a good scrub. My idea of bliss is to cook great batches of bread and pies and cakes and fill a freezer, so that I have loads to share with friends. When I visit my parents I do that and try all the local recipes, wherever they're stationed over the world.'

'Can you make a good jambalaya?' asked Dahlia wistfully. 'Creole cooking and fish dishes?'

'Hang on!' laughed Tricia. 'One thing at a time, but you never know, I might burst out into West Indian dishes another time. My father was in Key West in Florida, and we took a trip among the Islands after I'd stayed with him for a week. After this year, I hope to get a flat of my own and then I can please myself what I cook and what I eat.'

'And who you invite?' said Dahlia.

'That too, but I promised my parents to stay in the hostel for a year first.'

'Very wise. Come on back to work for another few hours and then get prettied up for Dr Jeffrey.'

'You've talked me into it, Nurse Stephens, and if it goes wrong I shall say I was obeying orders from a senior staff nurse!' laughed Tricia.

She pushed away the last of her meal and drank a glass of water, then hurried back with Dahlia just in time to see Mr Carter being wheeled into the ward. A theatre nurse held a drip bag aloft and a student held the loose end of a drainage tube that was sewn into the wound. It was already draining a small amount of dark ochre fluid into the bottle they now tied to the side of the bed, and the saline-glucose drip was adjusted to flow fairly quickly into a vein in his arm.

Sister nodded to the nurses and asked the staff

nurse for an aspiration syringe to clear the nasal tube that the anaesthetist had left in situ and which would be there for a day or so.

'Why does every surgical case have a tube into the stomach, Nurse?' asked Tricia. 'I can understand it when they operate on the stomach and in this case too, as he can't have anything by mouth for a while, but even the hernia cases had the same treatment.'

'Not many people are sick after anaesthetic now, but a tube makes sure that the stomach is empty and that gases can't build up and give them windy pains,' said Dahlia. She laughed, seeing that the junior nurse was slightly overawed by the sight of the very jaundiced man with tubes sticking out all over. 'Can't really pick him up and put him on your shoulder to tap his back as you would de-wind a baby, can you? This is a simple procedure to avoid distension, and if they don't need the tube once they're back in the ward, it comes out easily, as you know. It's easier this way than trying to make a fully conscious patient swallow a tube. Believe it or not, they aren't very keen on the idea! You removed one, and I can see there'll be others for you as you did it so well.'

'Don't!' shuddered Tricia. 'I hated it.'

'Take this dish, Nurse, and fetch more swabs, and then make up a mouth tray,' Sister ordered.

'Yes, Sister.' Tricia frowned in her effort to remember what she had been taught. She found a large kidney dish and put three small round gallipots in it. One contained glycothymoline to keep the mouth fresh, one a cluster of small wooden sticks with buds of cotton wool on the ends, and the other a weak solution of sodium bicarbonate to dissolve mucus. She added small swabs, and a pair of sinus forceps that could be used to grip the swabs if something bigger than cotton wool buds was needed. A small plastic cape and towel and a pot for dirty swabs completed the tray, and she took it to the bedside for Sister to inspect.

'Good! He'll have nothing by mouth for several days. A drip, and later the nasal tube will give him fluid which he badly needs as he's very dehydrated, but his mouth will need cleaning every four hours while he's on the drip or he could get an infection of his parotid glands.' Sister left the second-year nurse to sit by the bed and take a quarter-hourly pulse rate and made a quick round of the other post-ops. 'I'll have some tea in my office, Nurse Metcalf. I can't leave this lot just yet.'

From the ward kitchen, Tricia heard men's voices and saw that Mr Masters, Dr Clancy and the anaesthetic registrar were coming into the ward, so she added three extra tea-bags to the pot and put more water to boil to fill the biggest jug. The biscuit tin held only a very plain hospital selection and the cake had all gone. She carried the tray into the office, and Sister smiled when she saw the extra cups. 'I put more tea in the pot, Sister, but there isn't much to eat. Would you like me to fetch something for you from the cafeteria?'

'No, they'll have had coffee in the surgeons' room, and Sister spoils them with home-made cake.'

'I'd settle for a nice chocolate biscuit,' said Dr

Clancy, holding up a rather dry Marie biscuit. 'Nurse Metcalf has a huge tin that she keeps all to herself.'

'I try to,' Tricia replied demurely. 'But the moment I opened the tin all the best were taken.' She began to pour the tea after Sister asked her to do so, and handed the cups round. 'Sugar?' she asked, and held out the bowl.

'Thanks, honey,' said Dr Clancy, and she saw that he was laughing at her stony face. He took the bowl and his hand touched hers, his smile dying and an expression of reluctant awareness making him pause until Mr Masters asked for the sugar.

Sister Stafford looked at her watch. 'Check that Mr Bayard is all right and doesn't want anything, go down for tea, then tidy beds before you go off duty.'

Tricia escaped from the office, knowing that Matthew Clancy was watching her with an enigmatic expression which she found disturbing. He's waking up to the fact that I'm a woman and not a shadow of his sisters, she realised with a mixture of elation and an underlying fear. She joined Josie for tea and watched her munching a very large Danish pastry. 'It's all right for some,' Josie said enviously. 'I shall have to eat supper here while you're swanning off for dinner.'

'Has he told everyone we have a date?' asked Tricia, annoyed that her private business seemed to be common knowledge.

'No, you told me he'd asked you and I knew you'd go,' Josie replied calmly. 'Too good a date to miss. What are you wearing?'

'I hadn't thought,' said Tricia shortly. 'Does it matter?'

'If you wear something revealing he'll take it that you'll let him go that much further, and if you wear something ordinary you'll feel wrong and out of place if he takes you somewhere smart.'

'So what do you suggest?' Tricia asked with an ironic smile.

'With that one?' Josie grinned. 'I'd wear a leotard and tights and a high-necked sweater. Nothing like it for beating the odd fumble! On the other hand, quite a challenge, and men *do* like a challenge. He'd find it a turn-on.'

'You're no help at all,' Tricia said crossly, and hurried back on duty, but when at last she was in her room and gathered up her toilet bag and towel ready to go to the shower-room, she considered what Josie had said, and decided she had better play safe and wear a long plain skirt with a pretty but unobtrusive shirt tucked in and secured by a wide leather belt from Egypt that would look smart but understated.

She stripped and decided that her hair wouldn't dry in time if she washed it, then realised she had forgotten to bring a shower cap. 'Damn!' she muttered, and wished she were in her own flat where she could wander about naked if she needed to fetch anything. Her bath towel, strictly hospital economy issue, was adequate for drying but hardly big enough to drape carelessly round her body gracefully and seductively like the girls in the shampoo advertisements. She wrapped it round under her arms and held it together, peeped out to see that the corridor was clear and dashed towards her room.

From the floor below she heard the telephone ringing, but ignored it as she knew it wasn't for her. It stopped, and she found her bath cap and put it on so that she could have her hands free to hold the towel safely round her, then ventured once again into the corridor to go back to the shower-room. Footsteps on the stairs made her pause. The shower-room was nearer than her room now but the stairs led up to the corridor beyond the showers, and a quick dash was out of the question if she was to preserve her modesty.

She hesitated just too long, and the hurried athletic steps, taking the stairs two at a time, reached her floor. She froze, her legs unable to carry her further, as Matthew Clancy faced her just before she reached the safety of the shower-room. He stared and blinked as if he didn't believe his own eyes, then grinned, his gaze taking in every detail of the inadequate towel, the soft outline of her breasts under the tight fold of cloth and the slender legs and bare feet emerging from the emergency sarong.

'Hold it!' he commanded, and she saw with horror that he still carried his camera slung round his neck.

'No! Please, you mustn't!' she began, but the shutter clicked and her outstretched hand was of no avail.

'You didn't smile,' he accused her, and she was suddenly furious. He looked so pleased with himself, so sure he could get away with it and that she would think it funny.

'If you have that film developed, I'll. . . I'll——'
she spluttered.

'I said I wanted souvenir snaps of this place,' he
said. 'I shall treasure this if I can't take the original
subject with me.' His voice deepened and his eyes
lost their first gleeful triumph. 'I had no idea,' he
whispered, and came towards her, slowly as if a veil
had lifted from his mind.

'Keep away,' she whispered, but her mouth was
dry and she wanted the grey-green eyes to go on
looking at her like that and the firm arms to take
her, towel and all, into an enveloping embrace that
would last for ever. She gave a shuddering sigh and
felt the towel working loose. Panic-stricken, she
turned and fled to her room, and as she reached for
the door catch the towel slid away, leaving a vision
of peaches and cream and infinitely tender curves in
a ray of sunshine from the high window.

Angrily she zipped up a long housecoat and listened. There was silence in the corridor, and she
went back to the shower-room.

On her toilet bag she found a piece of paper torn
from a notepad. 'Sorry, but no, not sorry, and I love
the hat.'

She looked in the misted mirror and blushed with
shame. The very ornate shower cap, a cringe-making
present from a cousin with no taste, looked even
worse now, set at an angle with wisps of hair curling
out at one side. She turned on the hot water, taking
a masochistic delight in the stinging jet, then turned
on more cold water and soaped her body, breathing
in the scent that usually soothed her, of dark roses,

slightly bitter, from the toiletries that had been given her with the message that this was made from the original attar of roses used in the harems of the East.

She washed it away, but the elusive scent lingered, and she tried not to think of harems and naked girls being chosen to pleasure their master, but she felt she could never appreciate the voluptuous perfume again without seeing in her imagination the face of Matthew Clancy, laughing at her.

Why had he suddenly appeared in the hostel? she wondered. He had an apartment of his own somewhere up on the hill near to the hospital, and it wasn't likely that he had to visit another doctor as there were only three at present using the accommodation offered, none from his firm and none who were his friends. Most of the staff nurses lived out and some of the sisters, but the ones who remained because they were often on call had very nice flats on the upper floors, with their own bathrooms en-suite. Two of the theatre sisters lived in, and a senior nursing officer who preferred to live in but had a small cottage in Surrey for her off-duty weekends was on the top floor with views of the park. Ruth King also had a flat there, Tricia remembered.

She applied a touch of eye make-up and a trace of pale lipstick, then thought she looked too pale, so she wiped her lips and used a brighter colour. I need a date to restore my crushed pride, she thought ruefully, but she felt more like curling up with a good book, a few apples and a lovely wallow in misery.

At first she thought that Paul Jeffrey had forgotten

the date or had decided to stand her up, then she saw him lazily leaning against the wall of the car park, watching the doorway of the hostel. He walked slowly towards her and smiled. 'Slight snag,' he told her. 'My car has developed appendicitis or something equally unfortunate and had to be towed away rather ignominiously for treatment.'

'That's all right,' said Tricia. 'Another time, perhaps?' She tried not to sound relieved.

'Oh, no, just a change of plan. I tried to scrounge a car, but everyone seems to have his own date tonight. It's a fine evening for a walk if your shoes aren't too precious, and the Falcon's latest room is very good for dinner.'

'Great,' she said, with a bright smile, then wondered if Paul Jeffrey might be even more of a menace in the park than in a car. 'I'd like some fresh air, and Sister would be pleased as she lectures us regularly on the delights of innocent enjoyment in breathing the air of the great outdoors.' She laughed. 'As far as I know, she spends all her off-duty reading and chatting to her friends in overheated rooms!'

'What a waste, but on the other hand, who'd want to take her out cavorting in the country?'

'She's very nice,' protested Tricia.

'There are nice people, and those who have something extra. I'm greedy. I only ask out beautiful women.'

'And do they accept?' she asked.

'Yes,' he said firmly, and turned towards the drive leading to the gateway to the park.

Tricia almost stopped walking, but quickly

recovered her cool. He's had his car washed, was her first thought as she saw Matthew Clancy open the door of the car into which he had invited her when she was selling Rose Day stickers. Her second thought was that she disapproved of Sister Ruth King's choice of dress. It was a filmy short affair with shoestring shoulder-straps as if she was ready for dancing, a very smart dinner party or. . .bed! Ruth's hand rested on Matthew's shoulder as she turned gracefully to sit in the passenger seat, and she laughed softly up into his eyes.

Matthew smiled down at her, handed her a jacket that matched the dress and stepped back, closed the door and walked round to the other side of the car. For a second, he saw Tricia and Paul Jeffrey, and the smile died. 'Come on,' Paul said with a proprietorial air, and took Tricia by the hand. 'Let's explore the park.' He laughed. 'Poor Clancy, he doesn't have a chance of escape. What she wants, Ruth gets. I'm just relieved that the heat is off me.' His laugh sounded false, and Tricia glanced up at him, seeing a momentary glimpse of anger. 'We had a few dates,' he said as if an explanation was needed, 'but she's too demanding. She's applied for a job in Canada, would you believe?'

'When does she leave?' asked Tricia.

'Not yet. Dear Ruth will stay with her toe in the water over there and stall them until she knows if it's really going to work out for her. If not, she'll stay and make some other poor guy miserable, but she'll make it. She'll have him for breakfast complete with pancakes and maple syrup,' Paul added bitterly.

CHAPTER SIX

'GOODNIGHT, and thank you.' Tricia went hastily into the hallway of the staff hostel and shook the raindrops from her hair, but then realised that she was not alone.

'Any coffee?' asked Matthew Clancy, and went into the kitchen.

'You had two cups in the restaurant,' said Ruth. She smiled. 'Come up to my room and we can have some Benedictine. I'm afraid I'm out of coffee.'

'Tricia has some,' he replied calmly. 'I don't call those after-dinner cups real cups,' he added firmly. 'And I must check on a patient before I go to bed.'

Feeling like 'a little green berry with hairs', as her cousin said when talking about feeling as if she was playing gooseberry to a couple who wanted to be alone, Tricia found her coffee and set it to filter. 'I'll leave you to have coffee,' she offered.

'Biscuits?' he suggested with a sweet smile.

'Only hospital ones,' she said firmly, longing to get away so that she had no need to see the way Ruth King smiled at Matthew and touched him as if she owned him, and no need to see his sweet tolerant smile when Ruth made a witty remark.

'After saving you and Jeffrey from a soaking?' He looked hurt. 'Sudden thunderstorms can really make a person wet. How fortunate that we all chose to eat in the Peregrine restaurant at the Falcon tonight.'

'I thought you'd booked at Mario's in Chelsea,' said Ruth, rather crossly.

'I know you suggested that, but I might have to go back on duty tonight if something blows up. Some of the cases today were a bit on the serious side, and it's easy to be contacted at the Falcon,' he said gently. 'I thought I'd explained that very thoroughly,' he added with an edge to his voice which made Tricia feel more cheerful. The pretty, very diaphanous dress and the soft murmurings over the wine had obviously not been a complete success, and he was ready to move away, not to stay and make Ruth really happy.

'Only coffee whitener,' Tricia said brightly, sensing the tension as she brought in coffee mugs and sugar.

'You pour, and you might as well drink some of your own coffee,' Matthew said kindly, but in a tone that meant, drink some because I say so!

Tricia fetched a third mug and wondered how Paul Jeffrey was feeling. She smiled at the memory of his furious face when Matthew had blandly suggested that he might like to be dropped off outside his own flat up the hill, instead of having to walk in the rain, even though it was easing off when they left the Falcon.

The evening had certainly had its good moments, and the meal was delicious. Paul was interesting and amusing, and it was only when she looked across the room towards the table where Ruth sat with her back to them and Matthew Clancy faced them that Tricia felt embarrassed and rather sad. Ruth talked vivaciously with much gesturing of her pretty hands, and her bare shoulders gleamed softly under the rosy lights. Matthew listened soberly and ate as if he really enjoyed the food and needed it.

Maybe he hasn't eaten all day, Tricia wondered, and knew that this must be true. He's tired, she decided, but the frown that appeared from time to time was not exactly fatigue but as if he ought to be in another place. She forced herself to listen more carefully to the last story that Paul was telling her and to laugh as if she had heard it all and not lost the punch line.

'More wine?' Paul asked, but she shook her head. 'Ah, come on,' he insisted, and filled her glass, but she sipped a little and left it, having no intention of becoming slightly over the top as Paul was about to be. The thought of walking back through the dark along the unlit Victorian paths of the park began to take on a slightly frightening aspect as his hand slid across the table to take hers and his eyes shone with something more potent than wine. She tried to make her ice-cream and fruit salad last a long time, and said yes to coffee, although he hinted that he could have some in her room.

'You can't expect me to make coffee and wash up after a lovely evening. If I made coffee late at night I'd sit up drinking it and never get to sleep,' she said.

'Suits me,' he replied with a sensual smile that did nothing to lighten the coldness of his eyes.

'Also I have to be up early for duty,' she reminded him.

'Then why are we wasting time here? We could be all cosy and ready for bed back at the hostel.'

'You don't live there,' she reminded him. This was becoming difficult, and there was no doubt as to what he intended. She smiled. 'I must get my beauty sleep, Paul, but why not come for a meal one evening at the hostel? I have permission to use the kitchen, and the music-room is ideal for entertaining. It would be all my own home cooking, and real Brazilian coffee and brandy to follow.'

He looked at her in delighted surprise. 'It's a great idea, Tricia. I'm quite overcome. Would you really go to all that trouble just for me?' Her innate sense of honesty wanted to say that he wouldn't be the only guest, but she held back and smiled, then had no chance to answer.

'Sorry to break it up.' They stared at Matthew Clancy as he stood by the table. 'Listen to the rain! I saw you had no car tonight, Jeffrey, and I wondered how you could get Nurse Metcalf home safely without a drenching.'

'Ever heard of taxis?' Paul sounded belligerent.

'No need. I can give you both a lift back if you're ready now?'

'Thank you,' said Tricia, and stood up, determined to accept, even though Ruth looked as cross as Paul Jeffrey did. 'My shoes wouldn't stand up to puddles,' she added. 'Are you sure it isn't putting you to a lot of trouble?'

'I assure you, no.' Matthew beckoned to Ruth,

who seemed to have difficulty doing up the thin and inadequate jacket and shivered slightly as the temperature dropped. 'Ruth looks cold and I want to get her back to something warmer,' he went on.

'I'm fine,' Ruth insisted, and looked at Paul with a mixture of annoyance and wounded pride as if she wanted his attention as well as that of Matthew Clancy, even if she had no use for it. Tricia recalled that Paul had said they had dated a few times. So who finished it? she wondered, and fervently hoped she would never have to work in Casualty again while Sister King was in charge.

'More coffee?' Tricia asked as Matthew put down his mug.

He glanced at his watch. 'Is that the time? No more, thank you, I have to dash.'

'But, Matthew——' Ruth began in an aggrieved tone.

'Sorry, but I promised, and they'll think I've forgotten,' he said apologetically.

Tricia gathered up the mugs and the coffee pot and carried them to the sink unit. They can't even kiss goodnight while I'm here, she decided, but saw no way of escape before she washed up. The thought gave her no pain. She screwed back the top of the coffee whitener and smiled to herself. Paul and Ruth were so alike, and tonight neither had got what they wanted.

'I'm off on Friday evening,' Ruth was saying.

'So am I, but I have to go away for the weekend,' said Matthew. 'See you when I come back. Lovely evening,' he added as an afterthought, and left the two girls together in an uneasy silence.

'Well, I'm going to bed,' Ruth said savagely. 'Sometimes I think all that man wants is his rotten old house in Devon and a few slaves!' She smiled suddenly. 'It might be different when we get to Canada,' she said. 'I'm very adaptable, and he'll need me there for his work, apart from anything more.'

Tricia dried the same mug three times. So they were leaving together. Why fool yourself? she told herself severely. He may look at you with those wonderful but strange eyes as if he finds you desirable, but when it comes to a permanent relationship he'll choose Ruth, who knows him, knows his work and knows his family, and is ready to do whatever he wants, including slip into bed with him.

Canada was a long way over the ocean, and once he left England, he might never return. I must 'fill my heart with little things', Tricia quoted, and resolutely tried to plan her own weekend off, but it presented a void of very little things, unless she told Paul Jeffrey that she had two and half days off and nothing to fill them.

The outer door opened, and she glanced into the hall to see who was coming in from a day off, wondering if the rain had stopped, then she darted back into the kitchen, hoping to hide. Footsteps that passed the kitchen door and went towards the stairs made her look out cautiously in time to see Matthew Clancy reach the first steps. Tears filled her eyes. He was sneaking back to Ruth King after pretending to have more important matters on his mind than seduction. How they would laugh at her! she thought. The little nurse who was in the way but who now must be safely in bed alone, with no risk of intruding on their privacy. She put the mugs away and wiped the sink dry. More footsteps, coming down the stairs? Surely Ruth was not asleep or unwilling to open the door to the man she wanted to marry?

'Nurse Metcalf?' She started. 'Tricia? For Pete's sake, where are you?' the irritated voice demanded.

'Washing up,' she said, as if she had only just heard him.

He poked his head cautiously round the door. 'I thought you must be taking yet another shower,' he said, and grinned. 'Ruth gone to bed?'

'Yes,' she replied.

'I went up to the ward to give Mr Davies some prints I promised him, but forgot he went home this afternoon early as we needed the bed. You have his address, I believe? I haven't time to find his notes if they've gone back to Records.'

'I promised to let him have a few snaps too,' Tricia said. She was conscious of the hazel eyes watching her closely. 'I had some more taken off. They do a twenty-four-hour service at the local chemist,' she added; as if he didn't already know that, she thought.

'One of me with Nurse Allen?' he asked mildly.

She nodded, and lowered her gaze, going on hastily, 'I showed him pictures of the Victorian gazebo and the wall seats in the park next to the hospital, and he was intrigued and wanted some to go with a chapter in a book on Victoriana.'

'Why did you take them?'

'I love old places, and I can't agree that all of that period is too ornate or vulgar. Some of it is very graceful and shows their great love of nature and beauty.'

'I think you're right, and I hate to see these things destroyed. It's as if we destroy the old values too.' Matthew opened an envelope. 'What do you think of this place?'

Tricia smiled. 'Is this the manor house that Mr Masters was talking about to Mr Davies?' She looked up, her lips parted and her eyes shining. 'Mr Masters said one of his colleagues owned a small manor house. Is this place yours?' she asked with a kind of awe. She gazed at the colour print of an old house that seemed to smile in sunlight, the grey walls massed with ivy and a huge branching pale mauve wisteria dripping heavy pendants of flowers over gnarled wood.

'We've lived in Knoll Barton for a very long time,' he said simply but with a shadow of sadness. 'I played there as a child, my sisters were born there and my parents died there after catching a tropical disease when they retired and thought they'd explore the world. Ironic. They loved the place and realised when they were away on safari that no other situation would ever satisfy them as Knoll Barton did. They couldn't get back fast enough, but their contentment was short-lived, and they both went within a few days of each other.'

'How terrible,' Tricia said softly. 'But how lucky you were to have such a childhood, with such memories.'

'It was ordinary, but happy, I suppose,' he said slowly.

'Ordinary?' She smiled sadly. 'Safe and happy in one place with your parents and sisters, surrounded by love? Ordinary? Living there and knowing that every tomorrow would be the same and the same again and the house would remain solid and comforting.' She gulped and hoped he couldn't see the brightness of tears threatening to fall.

Matthew looked over her shoulder at the picture. 'Some say very ordinary and a millstone round my neck. I've been advised to sell it and keep just the cottage as a pied-à-terre when I'm in Devon.'

'You must never part with it,' she said with conviction, then realised that she had no right to express such an opinion.

He put a hand under her chin and turned her to face him. 'Thank you for that,' he said softly, and kissed her on the lips. This time, the touch was gentle and yet shattering in its tenderness, and she felt her whole body dissolving into a dream of sensuality. 'Tricia, you're not good for me,' he whispered. 'I know what I have to do, and you undermine my resolve.' He took another picture similar to the first from the pack. 'Here, take one and take an untorn copy of yourself, which is *not* for Paul Jeffrey,' he added grimly, then laughed. 'I'm sure he'd prefer one of the others that I took by the shower-room, but as yet I haven't had those developed, and I shall make sure I collect them personally to prevent them falling into the wrong hands.'

'You will tear it up?' she pleaded, without hope.

'You can't put back the clock, Tricia. It happened, and tearing up a picture doesn't mean it never happened. I remember it well.' Matthew grinned. 'Especially the hat. I'll show it to you if you promise not to touch it,' he offered.

'I didn't tear up the other one,' she said, but he shook his head as if that was best forgotten and walked quickly to answer the outside line of the telephone. Tricia watched him take the receiver as if convinced that the call would be unwelcome, then his face relaxed somewhat. 'For you,' he said.

'Tricia Metcalf,' she said, hoping Paul wasn't calling from his apartment up the road. 'Dad!' she almost shouted. 'Where are you?'

'Ship-to-shore telephone, so I mustn't take long,' her father said crisply. 'We're on the way home to dry dock and I have to see people at the MOD and then fly out to a conference of NATO. I shall be in Dartmouth on Saturday. Can you make the Angel for dinner?'

'Yes,' she said. 'I have the weekend off. The Angel at eight?' And can you book me a room on the Marina?'

'Fine—will do. See you, darling.'

'Well, hang up if he's through,' Matthew said patiently.

'I thought he was in Gibraltar,' she said, smiling happily. 'My mother is still in the South of France.'

Matthew eyed her with interest. 'My guess is, he's in the Navy? Travels here, there and everywhere? That explains a lot. Now let me think. The Angel? Not Islington and the theatre as they don't serve dinner there at eight, to the best of my knowledge. The only other place salty enough for sailors is the Angel at Dartmouth. Right?'

'Right! Do you know Dartmouth?'

'On my doorstep, give or take a few miles,' he replied, and his eyes seemed deeper set and as green as a dark leaf. 'When do you go down?'

'I can go on Friday night, look round the area like a real tourist and then meet him on Saturday evening.'

'Sounds great,' he said. 'Drive slowly.'

'I shall have to go by train or coach. Train, I think, as the coach stops at so many places and takes ages. Thank you for reminding me. I must get a current timetable.'

'Can you be ready by six? I can give you a lift to the station as I have to go that way.'

'That's really kind,' said Tricia, and her smile made her whole face light up and her eyes showed her gratitude. 'I shall have to take something fairly smart, which means carrying a fairly bulky case, as Dad's a stickler for neatness and the Angel is a very well known restaurant where many Naval personnel from Dartmouth College eat.' She made a face. 'He'll meet lots of people he knows, and I shall sit through dessert listening to what happened the last time his friends were in Gib or Oman or wherever.'

'I know the feeling, but you can just smile and

dream, can't you? I can be far away when I'm bored and still look fairly *compos mentis*. Just nod occasionally and they'll think you're very intelligent. Like now,' Matthew added as she nodded agreement. 'You'll also need clothes for walking, if you intend to scour Dartmoor,' he suggested.

'If I stayed for a week, I'd need the same amount of luggage,' she admitted.

'Don't forget your bath cap,' he said, and escaped before she could reply, leaving the photographs for Mr Davies on the table. Tricia smiled, went to her room and made a pack of the pictures and the ones that she had promised to give him, and addressed it to the patient who had gone home. The photograph of herself she put in a drawer, but she propped the picture of the manor house against her mirror. 'Knoll Barton,' she murmured, as if it was a familiar and dear place just because Matthew Clancy had lived in it, laughed there as a child and had the company of sisters and parents all the time he was growing up.

Tricia recalled her mother pointing out a house in a seaside town when they were driving through it, and saying, 'Don't you remember, dear? We lived there for almost a year,' as if that was a very long time to be in one place.

She felt restless and unable to sleep, so she turned out the clothes in her wardrobe and selected what she might need for the weekend. The jeans were almost new and would do for travelling and sightseeing with the fringed cowboy shirt and light tan suede anorak. Walking boots might not be right with the outfit, but on the train she could wear moccasins, although she knew she'd need boots over rough ground. Even if they were heavy, she could take a taxi from the railway station at Dartmouth to the hotel on the Marina where her father had promised to book a room.

She listened to the rain that had started again and shrugged. At this rate I'll have to take far too much, she decided, but she knew that wet clothes would spoil her weekend, so she put in an extra pair of culottes of bright orange, with a shirt that tied below her bosom and had a pattern of leaves and impressions of flowers in shades of green and lemon. Not for Papa, she decided with a grin, but smart and trendy enough for the hotel by the Marina where the yachties gathered.

Strip sandals to go with her smart clothes, and a pair of canvas loafers, filled the bottom of the case, and on top she laid the silk suit that would meet with her father's approval. The soft peacock greens and blues were her favourite colours and the knife-edged fine pleating of the full skirt would, she knew, flow gracefully in a whispering wake as she walked.

Sleepy at last, she went to bed, only to dream of being in a room where wisteria climbed up by the window, and when she woke the dream was still with her, as if that was reality and the fact that she had to go on duty after breakfast was the dream.

'Had a good evening?' asked Josie, her mouth full of toast.

'Er—yes, I suppose I did,' Tricia admitted, tearing her mind away from grey walls and mauve flowers.

'How was our blond bombshell? Well behaved?'

Tricia smiled. 'He had no choice. It rained hard and we had a lift back from the Falcon. Dr Clancy was there with Sister King, and he dropped Paul off first before taking us back.'

'So no chance of a bit of the other?'

'Josie! I don't go in for that!' Tricia protested. 'You should know by now. I'm off men, and in any case, I wouldn't want to be a one-night stand.'

'No, but he'd try it on, and he is a bit of all right. When's your next date?'

'I'm meeting a man in Dartmouth on my weekend off,' Tricia said sweetly. 'He rang last night, so if you see Dr Jeffrey, just drop a hint, will you? It might put him off.'

'You dark horse!' laughed Josie, bursting with curiosity.

'Calm down, it's only my father, but as far as Paul is concerned I have no intention of saying who it is if he asks me out on Saturday, as I think he might.'

'Lucky old you! I wish I had a glamorous family who'd scoop me up and take me to expensive hotels.'

'It doesn't happen all that often, and I do miss then when they're away for months and months,' said Tricia. 'I may go to Hong Kong for my holiday, but even that's uncertain, as they never seem to know if they can plan six months ahead.'

Sister Stafford soon dispelled all dreams as she set the two girls to bedmaking and the bedpan round, and when they went to have coffee and to tidy their uniforms it seemed that they had been working for hours. Mr Masters went through the ward leaving a trail of disaster behind him in the form of rumpled bedclothes and scattered notes, and the beds had to be tidied all over again.

Ivor was back in the ward, disgruntled because the chest consultant had strictly forbidden him to go near a canoe for the next three months, and yet the knee injury was almost a thing of the past, healed and flexible.

'Stop glowering at me,' scolded Josie as she picked up the magazines that had slid to the floor from his bed. 'I didn't tip you out into the river!'

'Sorry, Nurse, but it isn't fair! I had that championship in my fist, and now I can't compete until next year.'

'He said you could do other things to expand that lung, like tennis if you don't go mad at it, but you can't risk getting a lung full of slightly suspect river water just now.'

'I haven't got a partner for tennis,' he grumbled.

'I'd offer in the interest of science,' Josie said demurely, 'but I'd have to clear it with the powers-that-be as we aren't allowed to talk to you lot outside this ward.'

'You can't do that,' Tricia began.

'Why not? Ivor's almost a nutcase, and I believe the psychiatrists encourage staff to mingle and help rehabilitate those kind of patients. I shall suggest it to Sister, making sure I think she should be the one to do it, then she might even be grateful if I offer to try it for an hour on the hospital courts,' Josie laughed. 'Bad luck if she thinks it's her duty to help you,' she said to Ivor, and he looked apprehensive.

'I think that's an excellent idea, Nurse Allen,' Sister said when Josie suggested it. 'The surgeon wants him to exercise under supervision at first, and the physio girls are too busy just now with the accident cases. Sure you don't mind giving up some off-duty for a worthy cause to raise a patient's morale?' she added, her eyes twinkling. 'Not more than half an hour, very gentle stuff, and then bring him back to have his condition charted. Just a knock-up, really,' she added, and Josie stifled a vulgar laugh, and said she'd see what tennis rackets she could find in the locker-room.

'You'll raise his pulse rate far too much if you dress in that pair of shorts that *nearly* comes down over your behind,' Tricia warned.

'All part of the treatment,' Josie said piously. 'But really, he does need a lift or he might become a depressive. He's typical of manic people who are on top of the world one minute and down the next. His knee's as good as new, but he does need to breathe more deeply. He's lazy and won't realise that he'll get better fast if he sticks to the rules. Who knows, I may coach him for Wimbledon instead of canoe slaloming!'

Off duty, Tricia glanced at the packed bag standing open on a chair so that the silk suit wouldn't be crushed and sighed for sea breezes and peaceful surroundings. Paul Jeffrey was too busy to come up to the ward, and she kept well away from Sister King's department. At last, the letter to Mr Davies was posted, Friday came, a few more things were added to the case and the clock came up to the last half hour on duty before she could have a quick shower and dress before Matthew took her to the station.

'I hear you're going to Devon with Clancy,' Paul Jeffrey said, hovering outside the ward door to catch her as she left. She shook her head. 'Nurse Allen told me you were going to Devon to meet someone and Clancy is off duty too, so I drew my own conclusions, and I think I'm right.' He looked annoyed.

'Dr Clancy is giving me a lift to the station, and I'm going to meet my father,' she replied. 'I think Dr Clancy may be going to Devon some time, but not with me,' she added firmly.

The thundercloud faded from Paul's brow and he grinned. 'Just as well, or Ruth would kill you!' He considered her with jealous interest. 'I think I would too.'

'You sound as if you have a lot in common with Sister King,' Tricia told him, and hurried over to the hostel.

She picked up her duffel bag and case and looked back from the door to make sure she had forgotten nothing, then saw the picture of Knoll Barton propped up by the mirror. She slipped it into her bag and closed the door after her. I don't know exactly when the train leaves, but I think I have plenty of time to buy my ticket, she decided. Sister Stafford often went to Devon and had assured her that there was another later train that she could take if she missed the early one, so she felt relaxed.

Matthew Clancy stood by his car and took the

case from her. 'You decided to stay for a month, I see,' he said, and swung it into the boot by the side of a briefcase and a squashy bag that looked full. 'No umbrella?' he asked, with a quizzical glance at her suede jacket.

'In my duffel. It telescopes,' she said.

'What it must be like to be sure you have everything you need!' he sighed as he sat down in the driver's seat. 'I have no one to pack for me.'

'Nor have I,' Tricia answered, without sympathy. 'And I've been up to my elbows in nasties all day, but I did send off your snaps to Mr Davies yesterday. Did you know you left them in the hostel?'

'I thought you'd see to it,' he said vaguely, and eased the car out into the evening rush-hour. Tricia sat back and enjoyed the feeling of being free to have the whole weekend away, and to savour the fact that she was sitting close to the man she knew she wanted with the whole of her being, even though she could never marry him.

'Where are we going?' she asked suddenly. 'It's Paddington we need for the West Country!' Surely he couldn't be so stupid?

'Don't panic.' For a second his hand rested on her knee, then he steered expertly between two buses and emerged into a space in the traffic. 'Soon be out of this,' he said with satisfaction.

'We're nearly out of London!' she wailed. 'I shall miss my train!'

He laughed. 'I've done it! I've really done it! I've abducted a nurse from the Princess Beatrice

Hospital against her will. The ginger-haired maniac strikes again!'

'Take me back, or let me out and I'll get a taxi!' she stormed. 'I have a train to catch, and this is beyond a joke. I have to get to Dartmouth this evening.'

'And so you shall,' Matthew said placidly. 'Why sit in a draughty, smoky carriage if someone is kind enough to take you by car?'

'All the way?'

He glanced sideways and grinned. 'As far as you want to go,' he remarked, and she blushed.

'Dartmouth will do,' she said in a chastened voice. 'And thank you.'

'Sweet words!' He sighed. 'Does this mean we can be friends at last?'

'I hope so, but. . .'

'No buts. If it's any consolation, I owe you an apology. A student saw Ruth tear up that picture, and he was curious and glanced at it, but left it there when he saw Jeffrey coming into the office. He did see Jeffrey pick it up and smooth out the creases. The lower echelons of the students' common-room took bets as to who was in the picture.'

'Oh!' Tricia sank as far back as she could and hid her face.

'I think everyone has forgotten it now,' Matthew added, 'but I wish I'd never accused you, and the least I can do to make up is to deliver you safely to your father.'

'This is very good,' she admitted. 'I love motorways, and I think the bridges are graceful, not

eyesores as some say. In this light they look almost
too fragile for the loads they take each day.'

'The shrubs and wildflowers make the banks more
gentle, and do you see that kestrel hovering above
the bank? They find good hunting by busy roads and
never seem to notice the traffic any more. They're
safe from people on foot as walking is forbidden
there.'

The miles flashed by and they made no stops, but
as lights turned the motorways to strings of crystal
beads above a dark snaking river, they saw the coast
and soon dropped into the valley of the Dart.

'We made good time, and I'm hungry,' said
Matthew. 'We can eat at the Marina after you book
into your room, and then I'll get back to Knoll
Barton as I have a lot to do there.'

The car park was almost full and from the restaurant soft light filtered out through the long lace
curtains that gave privacy but didn't impair the view
of the harbour. 'I doubt if we can eat here,' said
Tricia. 'It looks very busy.'

'I rang through earlier today,' Matthew said casually. He grinned. 'I'm not that badly organised when
something is important.'

'Like food?'

'And other things,' he said, and she lowered her
gaze as his lips twitched with a kind of tender
humour, and she had the impression that he was
hiding a secret joke. 'We'll leave your bag in the car
until after dinner.'

'A single room was booked for me,' Tricia said to

the Marina receptionist. 'Name of Metcalf, for two nights.'

The girl frowned and consulted a list. She ran a red-lacquered fingernail down a column of names and then turned the page. 'Ah, yes,' she said brightly. 'One single for Saturday night. You were in luck, as we're very full just now.'

'Two nights, tonight and Saturday,' Tricia insisted. 'My father told me he'd book it for me.'

'Sorry, but no. Just tomorrow,' the girl said firmly.

''Fraid so, Tricia, but there was no point in worrying you,' Matthew put in.

'You knew?' She regarded him with horror. 'What am I going to do? I can't wander around looking for a hotel after dark, and my father isn't due here until tomorrow, so I can't stay with him, wherever that might be. How did you know, and why didn't you tell me?' she asked coldly. 'It just isn't funny!'

'When you had that phone call, it occurred to me that your father took it for granted you'd travel down on Saturday to meet him. You spoke for such a short time that a misunderstanding was possible, so today, when I rang for a table booking, I asked about your room and tried to get another night, but I was assured they were fully booked for tonight with yachtsmen who start a big race from here tomorrow, and who wanted a night ashore to meet up and have a good time.'

'Why didn't you tell me? I could have stayed in London until tomorrow,' she complained.

'And waste a day in Devon? Come on, I'm famished, we've both had a busy week and I've driven for miles and miles without even a snack,' Matthew replied plaintively.

'I must ring round to a few hotels first,' she said.

'Didn't I tell you? I did manage to get something fixed, so you can enjoy your dinner, and I'll get you safely there, as it's a bit out of town but the only place available.' He grinned at a party of wet yachts-men making for the hot showers and food. 'Let's get in there before the vultures eat it all!'

CHAPTER SEVEN

THE lanes were dark with early summer leaf and the subdued rumble of traffic from the coast faded as Tricia huddled back in the car and wondered where she was going. This isn't real, she decided. It's a dream ride, sitting beside the man who can make my whole body soften with longing and yet can make me so mad I want to hit him. I must have fallen asleep, and I shall wake up and find I've overslept and missed my train.

'Nearly there,' said Matthew.

'You seem to know where we are,' she remarked, as he paused by a crossroads with no signpost, then went slowly along a rutted lane, where at times it narrowed and the hedges brushed the windows of the car.

'I've been along here before,' he said lightly. She knew he was laughing softly, with a kind of joyful anticipation, and, without knowing why, she shared his excitement.

Away ahead, the outline of a building took shape and the trees parted to show a circular driveway with a statue in the centre flowerbed. Lights from two sets of windows indicated that someone was there, but there was nothing to show a busy hotel or guesthouse. Tricia recalled some country hotels, half empty, with bad food and service and a gloomy atmosphere, and she wondered why Matthew could get excited about a dark old hotel. At least I shall have a bed for the night, and he may be so glad to be rid of me that he can afford to smile now, she thought.

The scent of May blossom and wet grass made the night air fresh, and she took a deep breath. At least the air was good. Matthew unlocked the boot of the car and she took her own case, staring at the front of the building. The outline was oddly familiar and a break in the scudding clouds showed the small tower at one side and shining roof tiles. A shadow over the porch became a living tree with ghostly pale flowers hanging in heavy racemes over the grey stone walls, and she gasped.

'It's Knoll Barton!' she exclaimed, and saw that Matthew had his own luggage in his hand. 'I can't stay here,' she protested.

'Any port in a storm, as my granny would say,' he replied. 'I can take you back and tip you out on the sea-front, but I don't advise it, as it's not a nice place for little girls alone.'

Tricia bit back the remark that it might be safer there than alone with him in his own home, and she followed meekly as he opened the front door. Common sense told her that a show of temper would be useless, and when she crossed the worn stone threshold she was glad she had remained silent. A young woman came towards them and kissed Matthew warmly. She smiled at Tricia and held out a hand in greeting.

'Welcome to Knoll Barton,' she said. 'Matthew

told me you needed a room, and I'm sure you'd like to go there with your gear before coming down for coffee before bed.'

'Thank you.' Tricia followed her up the broad shallow stairs and into a dimly lit room. Her hostess switched on a light and flooded the room with pastel colours and the gleam of well-polished wooden panelling. The bedcover was turned back invitingly and frilled pale pink pillows made a soft nest. Country magazines and a cut-glass carafe of water sat by the bed. A half-open door revealed a bathroom with pink and grey tiles and matching towels, and the scent of lavender came, faint but comforting, as Tricia put her jacket on the bed.

'Matthew looks after the fabric of the Manor but leaves all this to me,' said the young woman.

'It's beautiful!' Her heartfelt response made the woman smile. Who was she? Tricia wondered. Not a housekeeper. Housekeepers didn't greet their employers with kisses. A wife? Had those strange green-hazel eyes held this secret so that even Ruth King had no idea that he was married?

'I don't expect Matthew told you about me,' the young woman laughed. 'I do know you're Tricia, but I had to ask him twice on the phone so that I could at least call you by name! I'm Maureen, his eldest sister, and I live here at Knoll Barton for most of the time when I'm not in Switzerland, where I have a design centre.'

'I knew he had four sisters, but I really don't know your brother well enough to be told much about his family,' Tricia explained.

'Is that so?' Maureen sounded surprised. 'I thought you must be old friends.'

'No, I'm fairly new at Beattie's and was away in the teaching block for most of the time he's been there. I think you're confusing me with Ruth King, who does know your family.'

'You're not a bit like Ruth,' Maureen said firmly. 'I've made coffee, and if I know my brother he's already raided the cake tin. I expect he ate a good meal and has now forgotten it.'

'Do you make him cake?' Tricia smiled. Another sister who spoiled the tawny-haired only brother!

'Good heavens, no! I can't boil an egg. When I come here, Mrs Penrose cooks for us, and we have a daily to keep the place ticking over all the time. In a way it's a kind of self-defence, as my mother was inclined to wait on all men hand and foot! We dug our heels in at a very early age as we could see that we might become slaves to my father and Matthew and the odd uncle or so who came to visit. Matthew knows we never cook for him unless he helps, and frankly, he wouldn't appreciate it if we tried anything complicated. My pastry is like lead,' Maureen added cheerfully. 'Can you scramble eggs?' Tricia nodded. 'Good. You're breakfast. I don't mind clearing up, but cooking, *no*! Matthew will be pleased. He adores scrambled eggs, but with me he'd have to put up with cornflakes and toast.' She looked at Tricia uncertainly. 'You don't mind, do you? Say if you'd rather not. We do our own thing here.'

'I'd love to,' smiled Tricia. 'I like cooking.'

'Unless you want to spend hours over a hot stove,

never tell a man you can cook or he'll make you do just that, for ever. You have a career that will take up your time, as we have, and even my married sister carries on with her work and has a nanny for the children, and a housekeeper. It works well.'

'I'm here for only one night, so that doesn't signify,' Tricia said, and began to enjoy herself. 'I can't make a reputation as a cordon bleu cook by making scrambled eggs!' I can imagine for one night that I'm here with Matthew, living in this lovely house together and even being loved here. Tomorrow he might ask me to walk over the moors with him, she thought, the dream taking over again. We might really get to know each other without the hassle of hospital ranking and the knowledge that at Beattie's everyone knows if you sneeze.

'Cherry cake this time,' said Matthew. 'Mrs Penrose has three cakes in her repertoire—cherry, fruit cake with lumps of citrus peel that could do with chopping more finely and a kind of soggy chocolate cake that clings to the teeth. All go down in the middle.'

'Wrong mixture and wrong oven heat,' Tricia said without thinking.

'She can cook!' His eyes widened.

'Only scrambled eggs, and not that if you bully her,' Maureen said calmly.

Matthew yawned and his eyes looked tired. 'Breakfast at nine if that suits you?' he asked Maureen. 'I have to go to Newton Abbot about the boundary fence and visit Clive at the new private hospital, but you could take Tricia back to

Dartmouth after lunch. I'll call for you at the Marina on Sunday morning, Tricia. We can stop for lunch on the way back to London.'

'I can take a train,' she began.

'No need. I like company while I drive,' he replied casually, and said a lazy goodnight before departing up the stairs.

'At least he doesn't want to drag you over a few bogs and down a damp gully or two,' said Maureen, not knowing that Tricia longed to do just that.

Bed was a haven, but her thoughts were confused. Tricia turned over to see the sky through the window and wondered if Matthew Clancy had any feelings. For once she had sympathy with Ruth King, if she was treated to the offhand acceptance of her presence when he wanted it and then was pushed aside when he had no need of her. Did this happen when he was in love? Or was he so self-centred that he never let his feelings get that far to make him a slave to a passion he couldn't control? But the memory of his mouth and the firm cleft in the masculine chin, the solid feel of his arms and the healthy male smell, reminded her that he was capable of deep feeling, real and lasting love, if only a woman could tap the source and make it flow.

She slept, and was awakened by a dawn chorus such as she had seldom heard in the past few years. She stretched lazily and found to her surprise that she was blissfully rested. The sun shone with more strength for the first time in weeks, and the trees outside her window made soothing murmurs, turning clean green leaves to the sun. She flung open the

window and her dream was complete. Under the sill
hung the sweet-scented mauve flowers, and the
rough wood curving down to the roots was strong
enough for a Romeo to climb.

She dressed and put on her boots. It was early,
and even if Maureen was serious about scrambled
eggs for breakfast at nine, there was a precious hour
to pass before she need come back to the house.
The front door was unlocked, and she wondered if it
had been like that all night, safe from any intruder,
with the trust and careless confidence of the countryside. Wet leaves brushed her cheek as she bent to go
under a low branch, and a mist rose from the
paddock beyond, as the sun rose.

Another dream, she decided, with the heroine
walking knee-deep in cloud, but where was the hero,
striding towards her to catch her up in a passionate
embrace?

'Hello.' The deep voice made her start. 'Up early,'
Matthew said with approval. 'Couldn't you sleep, or
are you like me, afraid to miss a second of being
here?' His eyes were sombre and he seemed to find
it hard to smile. 'This is the best time, unless you
choose the dusk, or midday in summer when the
bees are busy and I feel lazy and the fruit is ripening.
Even Mrs Penrose can't ruin fresh raspberries and
cream, although she does her best and frequently
stews them in vast quantities that nobody eats.'

'Does she make raspberry jam? That's useful if
you have a glut of fruit, and they freeze well, unlike
strawberries which go pulpy after being on ice.'

'My mother made raspberry jam,' he said, and his

face relaxed. 'She was a very good cook, which is why my sisters are not, as she never let them help her in the kitchen.'

'Did they want to learn?' asked Tricia.

'Not really; they were content to mess about with ponies and school activities, and she said it was her hobby as well as her work.' He laughed. 'I shall never forget Maureen's face when the vicar asked if she'd carry on the tradition of having an annual cream tea and charity stalls here, the year after my mother died. Poor man, he was so abashed by her vehement refusal that he hastily remembered another appointment and didn't come back. Now he takes it for granted that we're among the ungodly.'

'What a shame! I think country fêtes are fun,' said Tricia.

Matthew eyed her with benevolent humour. 'I discover fresh facets to you all the time,' he said. 'Next time you come, I'll introduce you to the vicar and he can tell you where you can go to buy candy floss and to guess the weight of a pig, if that's what turns you on, but please don't win it, as we gave up keeping pigs here about fifty years ago.' He turned back. 'You're cooking my scrambled eggs, remember?' His eyes laughed at her, but his hands were tender. 'I must thank you in advance,' he said, and kissed her softly.

'What if I burn them?' she murmured.

'I trust you,' he whispered, and kissed her again with growing passion, his hands moving in a caress over her body. Her lips felt like crushed rose petals as she responded and felt her body grow soft against

his hardening passion. 'Tricia,' he whispered, 'you're
so sweet. You have no right to look like that so early
in the morning!' He thrust her away. 'Damn it! As it
is, I have far too much to remember about this
place! I don't need you to louse it up too.' He was
gone, and Tricia sat for a minute on a damp log to
get back her poise, and to resolve that she must
never let Matthew Clancy take over her heart completely, however much he showed he wanted her.
She must force herself to know that his body desired
her but his mind ruled, and he would never say he
loved her.

'Right! Scrambled eggs, then back to normal,
whatever that might be where Matthew Clancy's
concerned,' she said with a resigned smile.

The kitchen was the sort of place where it would
be warm on a cold winter night with the wood-
burning stove lit, but now it was airy and the only
sign of the fire was a pile of logs in a wicker basket
by the hearth, and Tricia eyed the modern cooking
appliances with pleasure. There was room to move
and to chat to people while the cook worked and
produced delectable dishes, she thought with envy.
The big deal table was set for three, with blue and
white china and a thick wooden bread-board, honey
in a flowery pot with a china bee on the lid and an
odd assortment of breads that had come from the
village shop and had been chosen by Mrs Penrose.

Tricia took three thick slices of very white soggy
bread and toasted them, then split them and toasted
the soft insides until she had passable toast Melba,

which she cut into triangles and placed as an edging to each helping of creamy scrambled eggs.

'This is good!' Matthew exclaimed.

'Don't sound so surprised, Matthew,' said Maureen. 'Tricia is obviously a natural scrambled egg maker, but that doesn't mean you can expect even more from her talents.' She laughed. 'Be very careful, Tricia. My brother is the most devious man I've ever met, and if he wasn't my brother I'd tell him to go to hell at times,' she said affectionately. 'If he thinks you can cook, he'll make you feed him, and you'll hardly know he's getting his own way. He takes no notice of any of us, and each time I see him I plead with him to get his hair cut, but he comes here looking like an intellectual drop-out and says he has no time to get it cut. Can you persuade him, Tricia?'

'He's far too senior a doctor for me to have any influence over him,' Tricia said demurely, but she remembered the sensation of thick bronzy hair on her face when Matthew kissed her and decided that it was even more sensual than a beard. 'And I'm not a cook. I'm trying to become an efficient nurse.'

'A nurse who can cook? How long is your training?' asked Matthew.

'After this year, two more, unless I do midwifery after that,' Tricia told him.

'What a pity,' he said calmly, but his eyes seemed to mock her and look for a reaction that she might not want to show. 'I can't wait that long. If you had finals now, I'd ask you to marry me and come to Canada, but I just can't wait that long. It will have to be another person who can fulfil all my requirements.'

'Why not advertise?' demanded Tricia in sudden fury. 'Wanted! One doormat who can cook, look beautiful, nurse a ward full of arrogant men and be. . .' She couldn't bring out the words. He could take it as said that she meant this paragon must be a good lover too; fantastic in bed. 'Put it on the notice board at the hostel, and step back in case you're trampled in the rush!'

He laughed as if pleased with her outburst. 'I must go, if I'm to get everything done today. I'll pick you up at ten tomorrow and take you back to the clinical-room where you obviously belong.'

Maureen began to clear the table, refusing help. 'I said I'd do this,' she insisted. 'You cooked, I clear, then we'll go into Dartmouth and have a look round and have lunch before I leave you at the hotel. Take a walk if you want to, or sit and look at the magazines. Mostly country ones and the local Press, but they have a certain charm.'

Tricia sat on a wide window seat and leafed through a magazine, then picked up the local paper. The gossip column made her smile at the parochial accounts of people and places that might be familiar to the people living in the surrounding area but had no meaning for the outside world, then a paragraph caught her attention.

'What is happening to the ancient home of the Clancy family? Rumour says it is for sale, but a member of the family hotly denies this. However, the rumours persist. Mr Matthew Clancy, FRCS, is seldom there and may take up a post in Canada. His lovely and talented sisters work far and wide and have no real stake in the manor of Knoll Barton.'

It went on to describe briefly the fact that the farms had already been sold and the Manor now consisted of the house and outbuildings, a couple of cottages and about ten acres of pasture land with a woody copse and a stream.

'Mr Clancy is unmarried and his only married sister lives in Canada, so there are no family ponies to graze the lush acres.' There was a bad photograph of Matthew, taken when he was unaware of the camera, and a picture of Knoll Barton.

Tricia gazed out at the view and her heart ached. How could anyone who had lived here for so long give it up? Rumours started and often became fact, she thought uneasily. Matthew was going to Canada, or so it was said, and he fed the rumour by gaining as much skill as possible that would be useful in any backwoods situation. Maureen was in Switzerland for nine months of the year and flitted off to New York and London frequently, so she was almost a guest now in the family home, and the other sisters came only for short breaks when they felt a pull back to Devon.

There was another rumour that Tricia tried to push away as unwelcome and impossible, but it persisted in her mind. Ruth King had also applied for a job in Canada and was convinced that once she had Matthew to herself there they would become lovers and probably be married.

She piled the magazines neatly and went to her

room to pack the few things she had taken out last night. Maureen was ready to leave, and Tricia smiled when she saw the low-slung red sports car that drew up at the front door.

'Men hate it,' Maureen said airily. 'They try to carve me up on the motorway, but I have a few extra horses under my bonnet and can lose them fast. Put on a headscarf, as it's fine enough to have the top down,' she added. 'I love driving and wish I had time to go on a track, but I content mysef with fast cars which I can drive fairly fast here, but really fast on the autobahns in Germany, where they're allowed to go over the top.'

She drove skilfully, and Tricia wondered if all the family were as confident and talented in their several ways. Maureen parked in the hotel car park, while Tricia signed in at Reception and this time was welcomed with a pleasant smile and assured that her room was ready. She left her case and joined Maureen, and together they explored the pretty town which lay bathed in sunshine under the eyes of the fine sweep of buildings on the hill that made up Dartmouth College, where Naval officers had been trained for generations and still had a reputation world-wide.

The cobbled side streets led down to the quays, and any restaurants and cafés lucky enough to have a view of the deep harbour were already filling up with tourists sipping coffee. Private yachts glinted in the sunshine, their white hulls and shining decks giving a carnival air to the blue water. Larger sea-going yachts lay at moorings, swinging lazily, with their crews getting ready for ocean racing, and tiny dinghies with children in safety jackets kept well inshore and up the river.

'You have the best of both worlds here,' said Tricia, and sighed. 'I love the sea and the country, and I'd adore a boat of my own.'

'We have a mooring, somewhere along the river,' Maureen told her. 'I prefer cars, but Matthew used to sail a lot and we still have a boat, I believe.' She sounded as if it was quite normal to 'just have a boat somewhere', and a mooring in a town where they were hard to come by and very expensive to hire. 'We'll look at the antique shops and then find a small place for lunch,' she said. 'I have to do a bit of shopping to pick up some toilet things and few more anti-malaria tablets, as I'm due in the Far East next week and have started a course in advance as they recommend, but I need more to take with me in case I'm delayed there.'

They sat under an awning in a sheltered corner of the harbour and ate fresh local crab salad. Maureen was more anxious to know about Tricia and her family than to tell her what she wanted to hear— details of Matthew's earlier life, and whether he had ever had a serious love affair now or in the past. They found they had been to many of the same exotic foreign places and chatted like old friends, and it was with mutual regret that they said goodbye later in the afternoon.

'I have to pack for a trip to Birmingham tomorrow. If Matthew wasn't taking you back I could have done so, but I haven't a lot of room after

stacking the back with files and samples, and I really
need the passenger seat for my own gear.' Maureen
smiled and suddenly looked very much like her
brother. 'I did mention it, as we could manage, but
he refused to let anyone drive you back but him.'

'He likes company when he drives,' said Tricia.

Maureen laughed, and kissed her cheek before
she got into her car. 'When you know us better,
you'll realise that we're masters of understatement
when it comes to our feelings!' Her engine roared
and the car left in a flurry of glistening red, while
Tricia wondered what she meant.

'Now I have to concentrate on my own family,'
Tricia told herself, and tore her mind away from
manor houses, wisteria and a man who kissed her as
if he wanted her desperately, then left her to his
sister while he went away to talk about fences!

Her father arrived five minutes early, as she knew
he would do, and eyed her sleek silk suit with
approval. 'Can you walk in those shoes?' he asked.
'The Angel isn't far, but the road isn't good. Bring
an umbrella.'

'I'm fine,' she asserted, and smiled, aware of the
firm bond between them and the caring behind his
cryptic comments. He and Matthew have a lot in
common, she decided, then forced herself to forget
Matthew for the evening, but it was impossible.

'Have a good run today?' her father asked.

'I came down yesterday,' she replied, then
stopped, as she had made up her mind not to let him
know that she had had no room booked for the
Friday night as he would feel it was his fault. 'I

stayed with friends,' she added hastily, and tried to change the conversation, but he was curious to know who she had in Dartmouth that he didn't know. 'He's a doctor at Beattie's and was coming down anyway, so he took pity on me as I had a day to spare.'

'Where did you stay?' His glance was keen and penetrating.

'It's all right, Dad!' Tricia laughed. 'I stayed at his home, where his sister was a very adequate chaperon, if that's what bugs you! But I *am* a big girl now, and you really mustn't look like that whenever I mention a man.'

'Sorry, darling, but I see so much mayhem in the Navy that I tend to be protective out of turn,' her father explained.

'He's collecting me tomorrow about ten to take me back, and he's far too senior to think of me as anything but a very inadequate sluice queen,' she added, trying to forget that Matthew Clancy had also noticed that she was pretty and had a potential for love. 'I'm a kind of able seaman in rank, as far as he's concerned,' she added wickedly, 'and we all know that captains and ratings don't mix!'

'Cheeky monkey,' he laughed. 'How about a champagne cocktail to start?'

As usual Tricia enjoyed every minute of his company, and it was with mutual regret that he took her back to the hotel and left for his quarters as a guest of the College. 'I'll write to Mother as soon as I get back,' she promised him. 'Try to come back for a visit soon. I can book an apartment if you can make

the UK a base for a few months,' she added
hopefully.

'It will have to be a hotel as we can't stay for long,
but we may come in the autumn.' He sighed. 'We
both wonder if we should buy a place somewhere as
a base, but it's fraught with difficulties. Even a
cottage needs some trustworthy person to keep an
eye on it when we'd be away, and it wouldn't be in
London near you, but close to one of the Naval
bases. In any case, you wouldn't be able to look
after it for us, but your mother in particular has a
yen for a regular base where she can hang up her
hat.'

'This is a pleasant area,' Tricia said, but she knew
that if they came to live there on leave it might add
to her troubles, as her hospitable parents would
insist on getting to know Matthew and Maureen
once they believed they had been kind to their
beloved daughter.

'Ideal,' said her father, 'but too far for you to look
out for a place for us, unless you hear from your
friends of a cottage on the market.'

'Most unlikely,' Tricia said firmly. She recalled
the gossip column. If the Clancys sold the Manor,
and the cottages too were on the market, that would
be worse than anything. Her family might buy one
of the cottages and she would have to see the Manor
owned by strangers and probably altered beyond
recognition, with Matthew far away in Canada
where she might never see him again.

'Just an idea,' said her father, and dismissed it
from his mind, but that night, kept awake by a

crowd of lively yachtsmen triumphant after winning a race, Tricia longed to have her parents closer or to have someone to care for her and hold her close whenever she needed a broad shoulder of comfort.

'Ready?' asked Matthew, and took her case. It was just ten-thirty, and he seemed in a hurry to get away. Surely most of the Sunday traffic would be towards Dartmouth and they should have a fairly good run back to London? The fine weather had been only a promise of summer and had lapsed back into dull grey skies and a flurry or so of rain. Tricia ran quickly to the car, and Matthew slammed the door and ran round to his side to avoid the shower. 'The roads will be slippery,' he said almost to himself. 'I've told Maureen to be careful, but she likes speed. She's good, but there's a fool round every corner,' he added.

'Has she left?' asked Tricia.

'She has to call in to collect something from a friend, but she said she'll meet us for lunch at an inn where we've made a rendezvous many times, just before she branches off to her route.'

Tricia looked at her watch. 'In that case, we have lots of time.' She wondered why he seemed ready to leave so early.

'Yes, but I'd planned to show you something of my favourite county,' he said ruefully, and leaned forward to wipe the windscreen free of mist. 'Do we drive, or sit in a bar and watch the rain?'

'Drive, please. I can imagine what it looks like through the mist, and it's certainly prettier than

south-east London, rain or no rain,' said Tricia,
touched that he had thought of entertaining her.
'I'm glad we're meeting Maureen again. I really
enjoyed yesterday.'

'So did she. My sister doesn't like all my friends,
but she seems to approve of you in a big way,'
Matthew said, and laughed. 'I think she believes I
stand over you with a whip in hospital and make you
work far too hard. Little does she know how frightened the medical staff are when confronted with the
fury of a good nurse!'

'But you still leave your gown and mask and boots
where you take them off,' she accused.

'I hope you didn't tell my sister,' Matthew replied
in mock alarm.

They drove along the coast and looked over Start
Point, but the mournful cry of seabirds was the only
indication that somewhere out there was the wide
ocean, now hidden in mist, and Matthew seemed
preoccupied. 'Shall we get on and wait for Maureen
at the inn?' Tricia suggested at last.

'Yes.' Matthew seemed relieved. 'Let's go.'

The motorway was a slick of black that held
surface water and made fast cars aqua-plane and
throw up blinding sweeps of rain on to the wind-
screens of following vehicles, and Tricia sensed the
mounting apprehension in the man beside her.
Twice the signs set a limit of forty miles an hour,
and at one notorious danger spot, police cars and an
ambulance converged on a black saloon car that had
skidded off the road.

'Nearly there,' said Matthew, and relaxed as the

rain cleared enough to make only the slow sweep of the windscreen necessary. The curve of the motorway took them round a bend, and Tricia saw his hands on the wheel tighten and his knuckles whiten. The car almost stalled, but he recovered and indicated that he wanted to turn on to the hard shoulder—then Tricia saw it.

Traffic hurtled by, ignoring the mangled wreck by the verge, the red paint still bright and the wheels dark with rain. The car was on its side with one wheel slowly revolving.

'Oh, *no*!' Tricia whispered. Matthew was already out of the car and running. A police car pulled up and set its hazard lights flashing to protect the wreck and the parked car. Voices on the radio summoned urgent help, while Matthew pulled at the shattered door of the red sports car where it sagged over the figure on the wet macadam.

'Easy now,' he said in a controlled voice. 'Yes, I am a doctor, Sergeant. Nurse Metcalf, please tie her legs together above and below the knees, but don't move her. Use your belt and mine until the ambulance comes. Now, Officer, wedge that wood under the side so that when I let go she has room to breathe.' He let the metal rest on the wood and breathed deeply. 'Mo darling, can you hear me?' His fingers felt for a pulse and he shuddered with a relief that he could only now express.

'Is she alive?' the policeman asked.

'Yes, she's alive,' said Matthew. 'Where's that bloody ambulance?' He began to tremble.

'It's here.' Tricia took his hand and pressed it to her cheek. 'It's here, Matthew, and she's alive.'

She led him away so that the ambulance crew could get to the wreck and encase Maureen in velcro splints and a neck collar before they moved her like a stiff mummy into the ambulance. It was all done with quiet efficiency and without wasting a second.

'Give me the car keys,' Tricia said firmly. 'I'll bring your car and you go with her. I'll just follow the ambulance.' Matthew nodded as if unaware of anything but the figure on the stretcher. 'She was thrown out, and she isn't crushed,' Tricia went on earnestly.

Matthew climbed into the back of the ambulance. 'They'll want details of her address and where to find me,' he said. 'It will save time if you see to that.'

The police sergeant was businesslike. 'That would help,' he agreed, and Tricia watched as the ambulance sped away along the motorway, then supplied all the information she could, adding that there would be no one at the Manor to contact and that Dr Matthew Clancy, based at the Princess Beatrice Hospital, was, as far as she knew, the next of kin.

'No, we didn't see the accident, but we arrived about the same time as the police car,' she said. He wanted to know who she was and where she lived, and it sounded as if she and Matthew lived together, until she assured him that he had been giving her a lift back to London after she had visited her father in Devon.

'Know the family well, miss?'

'No, hardly at all, but I did meet Miss Clancy yesterday and we had lunch together.'

'Nice new car. Has she been a driver for long? Would you say she was careful?'

Danger bells rang in Tricia's mind. What she said could be important, then she smiled. 'She's a very good driver. I felt completely safe with her, and she's a member of the Advanced Motorists, or whatever it's called. She's proud of that, and I can only think that she skidded or that someone carved her up and forced her towards the hard shoulder. She complained yesterday that it does happen and that some men hate women driving fast cars as it gives them an inferiority complex.'

The sergeant closed his notebook and spoke into his radio. 'You could be right, miss,' he said at last. 'A witness saw a car driving badly and sounding his horn at this red car and driver a few miles back in a manner that could be classed as harassment. We have a description, but we may not be lucky enough to catch him.' He smiled. 'Driving on to London now? Sure you feel OK?'

'Can you tell me where they took her, as I said I'd follow with Dr Clancy's car?' asked Tricia.

Once more he radioed, and nodded. 'Penmare Cottage Hospital is the nearest, so she's there until they find out how badly hurt she is. You leave the motorway at the next junction and strike off to the left, and it's a few miles along a B-road.'

'Thank you. May I go now?'

'Yes, miss, and I hope she isn't badly hurt. Nice-looking woman. Take care now.'

Tricia braced herself to drive an unfamiliar car and tried to recall which controls were in what position. She waited until a gap appeared in the traffic and started off slowly, then gained confidence and found that the gear change was similar to one she had used in France. The exit sign appeared and she left the busy road and paused at the roundabout.

Bear left, the man had said, but he had made no mention of roadworks, and a new lane led cars round the half-finished stretch. She looked about her, but the workmen obviously had Sunday off and there were no pedestrians about. 'Ah well, this is left,' she decided, and drove on past small houses and a farm, then stopped to see if there was a map in the glove compartment. Almost guiltily, as she hated rummaging in a car that didn't belong to her, she lifted out a sheaf of papers and found the map under a transparent plastic folder of photographs. She stared. Through the glossy film, Sister Ruth King smiled up at a man in brief swimming trunks. His arm was about her shoulder and he was laughing. Ruth was almost dressed in a very brief bikini and her hand rested on his bare chest in a way that said, I want you. You're mine.

Tricia found the route she needed and drove slowly to the hospital, anxious about Maureen but with a heart cold and sad. How could I ever fool myself? she thought. Ruth King looks like the cat with the cream, and what she wants, she gets.

CHAPTER EIGHT

'I SHALL stay, of course,' Matthew said. He ran his fingers through his hair and looked sombre. 'She's badly concussed and shocked, but blessedly, no bones broken and only a dislocated shoulder that we reduced while she was deeply unconscious. She recognised me and she wasn't unconscious for long enough to make us anxious, but she's best left here as they seem to know what to do.'

He became aware that Tricia wanted to tell him something. 'I gave the police all the information they needed and suggested that Maureen had been forced on to the hard shoulder by some maniac,' she said. 'The police sergeant checked reports of a man doing just that to a red sports car a few miles back. The timing tallies, so they're satisfied that Maureen wasn't driving carelessly.'

'Clever girl,' said Matthew. 'If we'd left it until later they might have forgotten the link and accused her of driving without care.'

'I have to get back to London,' she said. 'I can take a taxi to Exeter and then the train.'

He nodded as if dismissing her and reached for his diary. 'Tell Jeffrey I can't give gas in Casualty tomorrow, and leave a message for Boris that I may be here for the next day or so.'

'I'd rather you wrote notes,' Tricia said nervously.

'You forget I'm a junior nurse and can't just go up to consultants and give them verbal messages.'

'And you don't like the idea of being my secretary?'

'It's not that,' she began, but he shrugged and took out a notepad.

'Here,' he said at last, and asked a nurse for envelopes. Tricia took three notes, one for the consultant anaesthetist, one for Paul Jeffrey and one for Sister Ruth King. 'We'll check on Maureen and then I'll drive you to Exeter,' said Matthew.

'I can take a taxi,' she protested. 'It can't be very far from here.'

'I seem to have heard that before,' he remarked with a slight smile. 'Is there nothing you'd rather do than accept a lift from me? I'll take you to the station, but you needn't feel I'm doing you a favour, as I intend going on to the General Hospital where they have telex facilities and I can send a telex from there to Maureen's boyfriend in Switzerland.'

'I didn't know. . .'

'She doesn't talk about her private affairs a lot, but he's a good guy, and I hope that after this, she'll decide that life is short and she ought to get married. It's been a great shock. There'll be a lot of rethinking to do for all of us.' Matthew avoided her eyes. 'Ready? We'll take a peep at my sister and then go at once.'

Maureen lay quite still, but her eyelids flickered as Matthew said her name softly. She opened her eyes and saw him and smiled, then smiled at Tricia too. 'Stupid cow, aren't I? How did it happen?'

'It wasn't your fault,' Tricia said firmly. 'The police know that now.'

'Will Karl come over?' Maureen asked anxiously. 'I want to see him.'

'I'm going to telex him now. I'll stay until he takes over,' Matthew assured her.

'Great,' Maureen whispered, and closed her eyes.

'Come on,' Matthew said almost impatiently, as if he didn't want to be reminded that Maureen was coming to terms with being deeply in love.

'I'm ready.' Tricia put the notes in her bag and followed him to the car. The rain had stopped, but the countryside looked beaten down and sad. Goodbye, Devon, Tricia thought sadly. What shall I remember most, the pretty room where I slept in Matthew's home, the dinner with my father, or the sight of Maureen lying helpless and still by a wet roadside?

She glanced at Matthew's set face. A deep line had formed between his brows and he looked tired. She longed to make him stop the car and to cradle him in her arms, giving him anything and everything he wanted from her, but he drove on silently, with an invisible barrier between them, detached and formal, the fine web of sensuality torn and any accidental touch without magic. Was it only Maureen who had to do a lot of rethinking? Tricia was increasingly depressed. That note to Ruth King might be anything, from a bare piece of information about Maureen's accident to a declaration of love as Matthew came to terms with his future and knew he needed a wife to be with him always.

'I think the trains run fairly frequently,' Matthew said when he turned into the station approach. 'If you hurry, you might catch one now, as I know that one goes twenty minutes before the hour.' Hastily he handed her the luggage and kissed her on the cheek, as if he was seeing a cousin off on the train. A cousin, Tricia thought, with whom he didn't want to linger over goodbyes. 'See you soon,' he said. 'I have to sort out a lot of things and make sure Karl knows as quickly as possible.'

Tricia bought her ticket and went to the right platform. Was this to be another sad memory? The smell of a railway station and the distant rumble of wheels on rails as the train came round the bend, and nobody to say goodbye to her with warmth and love as if full of regret that she had to go?

When she was on the train, she realised she was hungry and there was no buffet car. No lunch, no sunshine, no drive back with Matthew, and no hope of his love. The note to Ruth seemed to burn a hole in her purse. He had thought of Ruth King the moment he had a crisis and sent her a letter.

Paddington Station bustled with anonymous people and the queue for a taxi was long, but at last Tricia was back within the gates of the Princess Beatrice Hospital, and it was like coming home after a funeral. 'Stop it!' she told herself angrily. 'You like your work, you have friends here and you're planning a party.' A party? The sudden change of plan that took her to Devon had driven out the idea, and yet she had an uneasy feeling that people would be expecting food tomorrow evening. She had wanted to cook and have the party on the same day, but Monday night had been suggested as a better night to have the music-room private, and she had meant to cook on the last day of her weekend off, which she now realised was today!

It was still early, and Tricia made coffee and ate a handful of biscuits before putting red beans, which had been soaking in cold water in the fridge, with onions and tomato puree to simmer in the biggest pot, with garlic and herbs and some sliced sausage and pieces of pork. She walked over to Casualty and was relieved to see that the staff nurse was in charge. She asked her to bleep Dr Boris and tell him that a note awaited him there.

'He's at home, but Sister will take the note and give it to him in the morning,' said the staff nurse.

'Dr Clancy sent notes for Sister King and Dr Jeffrey too,' Tricia said.

'Sister is with Dr Jeffrey now,' the nurse said. She raised her eyebrows. 'Closeted in the office over gallons of coffee. Will you disturb them or shall I?' She took the notes. 'What's happened to Dr Clancy? Couldn't he give them his own messages tomorrow when he gives the three gases?'

Tricia told her briefly what had happened. 'So he's staying on until he's satisfied that Maureen is better. You'd better see them, as Sister made a fuss the last time I came in here out of uniform.'

'Not today! She heard that she has the job in Canada in a new hospital, starting in four months' time, so she's on top of the world.'

'I see. Must go—I have a pot boiling on the

stove,' Tricia said incoherently. The girl stared and laughed.

'Cooking for me?' Paul Jeffrey came up behind her.

'Tomorrow evening in the music-room,' she said. 'My little party.'

He took the note that the Casualty nurse handed him and opened it. '*Our* little party?' he asked softly. 'Do I bring champagne?'

'No, we're drinking cider,' Tricia said firmly, and turned to go.

'Hell's bells! Who does he think he is, sloping off when I need him?' Paul looked angry as he read the brief note.

'There's a family crisis,' the nurse told him, and winked at Tricia. 'Maybe his wife's expecting a baby or his grandfather's died.' It was evident that Matthew Clancy saw no reason to confide in Dr Jeffrey and had made no allusion to the accident, and neither of the girls explained what had happened.

Tricia slipped away back to the stove and made pastry for a large vegetable flan and checked that the list of fruit and salad vegetables was complete so that Josie, who was off duty in the morning, could do the last-minute shopping.

In spite of her heavy heart, she took solace in cooking, and when she had eaten supper in the staff cafeteria she felt better. I was just famished, she decided. That's why I felt so depressed. She wondered what had been in the note for Sister King, and tried to be fair. Ruth King was a friend of the family as well as being Matthew's colleague and even closer friend. Maureen might appreciate a visit from her before she went back to Switzerland, so there was every reason for Matthew giving her the news.

The cassoulet had cooled overnight and was in the fridge ready to re-heat for the party, the flan had turned out well, with featherlight pastry and a luscious filling of vegetables in a cheesy sauce over a base of asparagus, and Josie had gone out armed with a huge carrier bag and a list. Tricia tried to concentrate on her work, and Sister Stafford had to ask her twice to tidy Ivor's bed.

'Is something wrong, Nurse?' she asked.

'I suppose I still feel a bit shaken, Sister,' Tricia said, and told her about the accident.

'Well, hard work is the best cure for that! Take these X-rays down to the department and collect the special packet from Dispensary that Mr Masters ordered, then report back to me and come with me on my next round.' Tricia turned to go. 'And, Nurse—don't take it so much to heart! Accidents happen, and you're privileged to help with the special skills that you're learning fast. No experience is wasted, and you'll be glad one day that you had Dr Clancy with you to show you what to do. It must have been tough on him to have to give first aid to his own sister without the facilities of a hospital.'

'He made sure that she had room to breathe, and we tied her legs together to help immobilise them in case she was moved awkwardly and there was something broken,' Tricia told Sister. 'Then the ambulance men came with the right equipment. They were wonderful!'

'So Dr Clancy was giving you a lift?'

Tricia sighed inwardly and knew that soon the whole of Beattie's would know that the good-looking doctor had taken a first-year nurse to Devon for the weekend, so she told Sister Stafford he had been kind enough to give her a lift to Dartmouth on his way home as she had to meet her father there. It was the bare truth, and she hoped there would be no need for further explanations, like where she had slept the first night or how she had enjoyed being a guest in Matthew's house.

Ivor was sitting in the day-room, annoyed that Josie had deserted him for the morning, and had no time to give him half an hour on the tennis court. 'It's part of my treatment,' he said self-righteously. 'The doc says my chest is much better after filling my lungs with air a few times.' He looked at Sister Stafford with exaggerated pathos as she checked his pulse.

'Very unorthodox treatment,' she said primly. 'In my day no nurse was allowed to play games with patients outside the ward.' Tricia noticed that she was trying not to smile. 'However, I agree that it's done you a lot of good, physically and psychologically, so I've arranged something for you. Be ready in ten minutes and you shall have your half-hour.'

'You mean Josie. . . I mean Nurse Allen is coming back specially?' he asked eagerly.

Sister smiled enigmatically and noted his pulse rate on the chart, then his respiration rate, observed when he was unaware of her being there. 'Much better. I think Mr Masters will let you go home soon.'

'I'm not entirely fit yet, Sister,' Ivor pleaded.

'Fit enough for most activities, I'd say,' Sister remarked drily, and he blushed. 'Now get into your tracksuit and wait here.'

'Nurse Allen has gone shopping,' said Tricia when they moved on to the beds in the ward.

'I know,' Sister Stafford chuckled. 'That lad has a bad case of nurse fixation! He'll get over it when he leaves here, but it's acute while it lasts and the patient thinks it's real at the time. I know all about that, and nurses must never take it seriously or it leads to a lot of heartache.' She eyed Tricia with speculation. 'I hope Nurse Allen hasn't any plans for meeting Ivor once he leaves here? It's not a good idea, and often when we see patients dressed to go home, they suddenly appear like strangers. We know more about their bodies than perhaps anyone will ever do for the rest of their lives, except a wife or husband, and yet we have no real bond with them apart from service and gratitude.'

'Nurse Allen has a regular boyfriend, Sister. She likes men, but she isn't falling for Ivor,' Tricia said firmly.

'Well, here's his tennis partner,' Sister Stafford laughed. 'He's the new physiotherapist who deals with all the hydro-therapy, and he jumped at the chance of trying tennis as a recuperative aid.' The wide-shouldered boy grinned. 'He's behind those curtains, changing,' Sister told him. 'Nothing too rough! He's not fit yet, but I think that after this morning Ivor will want to go home as soon as possible!' She left them to get sorted out.

Mr Carter sat up in bed with the tube from his gallbladder operation still draining a few drops of less dark fluid now into the bottle tied under the bed, and his jaundice had almost disappeared. 'They're bringing a portable X-ray to the ward to take pictures,' Sister said cheerfully. 'Any pain?'

'I feel much brighter altogether, Sister. No pain after that last bout when a lot of grit came down the tube, and it's not sore round the wound now.'

'If the X-rays show no more grit or stones, then I think the tube will be taken out. I see from your intake chart that you're drinking normally and keeping up a good fluid intake, which will make you better very much faster than if you didn't drink.'

'I took a look in the mirror and I think the yellow is almost gone. It wasn't nice, looking a bit like a lizard,' Mr Carter smiled. 'Even the whites of my eyes were yellow! I really do feel better, and I can think of doing a lot of things that I couldn't face before my op. I might even take the wife to Spain as she's wanted me to do for ages, as soon as I'm fit.'

'All those bile salts free in the bloodstream, making him jaundiced, also made him very depressed, and he's coming out of that nicely,' said Sister, as soon as they left his bedside. 'He'll feel better than he's done for years and be able to eat anything he likes, instead of being nauseated by anything fat, like milk, butter and cheese, but I hope he keeps off animal fats, as he does have a high cholesterol level at present.'

Tricia made up a bed ready for a new patient as soon as Mr Mark, one of the hernia cases, had been taken home by his wife to convalesce, with the warning that he must lift nothing heavy for three months but otherwise live a normal existence and take plenty of gentle exercise. The other hernia case, Mr Jenkins, grumbled that he had been to the theatre at the same time and was still feeling unwell.

'You have a very nasty cough,' Sister said firmly. 'We must see what the chest X-rays show before we can discharge you, as you may need further treatment.'

'Do you think he's really ill?' asked Tricia when they were back in the office and Sister Stafford held up the X-rays to the brightly lit viewer.

'Mr Masters will want to see them before he decides what to do, but I think that after a lifetime of smoking Mr Jenkins has chronic bronchitis which could lead to something far more sinister. Physiotherapy and good diet with no smoking might save him, but that depends on him.' She sighed. 'Some people think they're immortal and can do what they like and never be really ill.'

Tricia had vivid recall of the accident. Maureen must have felt immortal until the accident. She was one of the beautiful, intelligent and prosperous people with everything going for her one minute, and flung out of a car the next, to lie like a rag doll in the rain. She also thought of the strained and shocked expression on Matthew Clancy's face as he came to the conclusion that it was not only hospital patients who suffered and died. Tragedy could touch him and his family, and maybe the time had come to make a secure and loving future for himself, with the responsibilities of his own family.

'Go for a break now and then help Nurse Stephens with dressing trolleys,' Sister said. 'You're off duty this evening, I believe. What have you planned? I suggest you do something definite and not sit alone and go over the events of yesterday.'

'I have permission to cook in the hostel and I'm having a small party, Sister. I arranged it before the weekend and I've done most of the cooking. Nurse Allen is buying the salad and bread sticks and cheese.'

'Have you enough plates? Why not use disposables?' Sister laughed. 'No, don't look alarmed— I'm not suggesting that you buy a lot of expensive things, but we had a garden fête last summer and have dozens of paper plates and mugs stacked up in my spare cupboard that were left over, and you're welcome to help yourself. There are plenty of plastic forks too. After the party they can all be put out as rubbish in a black plastic sack.'

'I wouldn't need many,' Tricia said uncertainly. 'Or at least, I don't think so. I've invited any staff I worked with on Gynae and Children's and of course this ward, and Dr Jeffrey is coming.'

'My dear girl, they'll turn up in droves! Word spreads, and you'll find people there whom you've never even met, let alone worked with!' Sister gave her a keen glance. 'I suppose Paul Jeffrey invited himself?'

The corners of her mouth twitched as Tricia

replied, 'I invited him in return for dinner one night, and I don't think he's heard that this is a real party.'

'He'll arrive with flowers and wine and that look in his eyes!' Sister Stafford laughed. 'Good for you, Nurse. I promise not to breathe a word if he comes up here to talk to Mr Bayard. He's really very good about that, and I leave a list of questions I want answered so that he can sort them out for me. I might even pop in later to wish you well and bring anything edible that I can get if you're running short of food. We had wonderful parties here when I was a student nurse, but now that so many live away from the hospital, they rush off home and we lose that social atmosphere. I remember Dr Boris playing the piano at musical evenings. He's a wonderful man,' she added with a look of pure nostalgia, then came back to the present. 'Get off now to coffee, as we may be busy later,' she said.

'I think I've got it all,' Josie told Tricia when she came back on duty. 'I also bought a tin of biscuits which you can have as a birthday present from me. Shall I make garlic bread as soon as I come off duty? It fills a hole, and I for one could eat lots.'

'I hope we have enough food,' said Tricia. 'Sister Stafford thinks a lot of people might come, including her, would you believe?'

'You made gallons of cassoulet, and if you put some aside for latecomers who can't have the evening off, you can see how many come early, and ration them to one helping each or they'll pig it all!' Josie said. 'They can fill up on garlic bread and cheese, and you do have a huge flan, remember, and enough salad to feed all the rabbits in Australia!'

'We have to tidy up before visitors,' Tricia said. 'So far, no new admissions, and we're fairly slack, so you might get off early tonight.'

'How's my friend Ivor? Did he miss me?' asked Josie.

'He had a very energetic physio guy to play with him for his tennis session, and he didn't like it at all! Most of the time was taken with breathing exercises, and Ivor prefers pretty nurses to butch giants, so he's changed his mind about going home and will be discharged on Wednesday.'

'In a way that's sad, as we get on well, but I'm really glad, as he was becoming a bit heavy,' said Josie. 'I find endless talk about canoes a bit limiting, and no, I don't want to accept his warm invitation to spend a day on a wet boat, practising capsizing!'

The rest of the day passed quickly and Tricia was busy enough to forget her own emotions. The party took up most of her thoughts, and when she went off duty she rushed over to the music-room to make sure it was free, then put the paper plates and cups and plastic forks on the long table by the door. Cider bottles and soft drinks with jugs of water took up a lot of room, and she dragged another table close to make a buffet. There was time to spare now, as the cassoulet was simmering gently to re-heat thoroughly and the flan was in the oven ready to heat later.

To her grateful delight, she found that Josie had washed all the salad and it was in a huge mixing bowl under clingfilm, so she went over to the phone and rang the cottage hospital in Devon where Maureen was a patient.

'Yes, I was there at the scene of the accident,' she explained. 'How is she?'

'Much better and almost ready to leave us,' the sister said. 'Obviously very bruised and sore, but should be able to travel in a day or so if she's careful and has someone to look after her. I think her brother will see to that.'

'Is Dr Clancy there?' Tricia asked, then wished she had made no mention of him as she couldn't think what to say if he came to the phone.

'No, he left earlier,' Sister told her. 'As soon as Miss Clancy's fiancé arrived he said he had to go home and then settle some urgent business, but he'll be back soon.'

'Give Maureen my love and say I'm very relieved that she's better,' said Tricia.

At least I shan't have the feeling that Matthew will suddenly appear, she thought. He may even go to Switzerland with Maureen or just go back to the Manor to help her pack her clothes, but he'll be away for a while.

The food smelled wonderful, and at half past seven there were nurses sitting waiting for the party to begin, but Tricia tried to stall them until the ones on duty for the evening were free. Josie came off duty early, thanks to Sister Stafford, and set out salad, advising a start to avoid everyone wanting to be served at once.

'What goes on?' His voice was amused but tinged

with annoyance, as Paul Jeffrey arrived, as Sister had suspected, with flowers and a large bottle of wine.

'Please come in,' Tricia said warmly. 'The party can really begin now you've arrived. Cassoulet or asparagus flan?'

He grinned, and whispered, 'Cunning bitch!' then decided to enjoy himself. 'Cassoulet *and* garlic bread? Great!'

'I hope you put some aside for us and for a few late off duty,' said Josie.

'Quite a lot, and we seem to be doing well,' Tricia said.

One of the male nurses went out for extra cider and Coke, and several others had brought wine and beer. A technician who lived close to the hospital with his family gave Tricia a fruit cake, and when Sister Stafford arrived she looked about her with approval. 'You put us all to shame, Nurse Metcalf! It's obvious that this is a great success, and we ought to have more get-togethers as some nurses don't have a great social life, living in bedsits.'

'I'm starving!' Josie said at last. 'They're all clacking away as if they'd never met before, so we can slip into the kitchen and eat our supper in peace. You go and fill a couple of plates while I go to the loo. See you in five minutes—and *don't* let anyone eat my share!'

The kitchen was empty, and Tricia looked into the reserve pot and stirred the contents, suddenly tired but elated. It was good to feed people, as well as to nurse, and she brushed back the curling hair that felt damp in the steam of the cassoulet. She looked up into the hazel eyes that she remembered so well, and heard the deep voice she had come to love.

'Not just scrambled eggs?'

She shook her head and blushed. 'I confess—I love cooking.'

He took her plate and fork. 'And I came just in time,' he said, and grinned. 'Thank you. Just as I like it! We make a good team. I like eating, and you like cooking.'

'Fortunately there's enough for you, as well as for Josie and me, who've been labouring over a hot stove for hours!' Tricia filled another plate and perched on the edge of the table, aware that he was watching her. 'I rang to enquire about Maureen,' she said to break the silence and the tension she felt growing between them.

'She was better as soon as she spoke to Karl on the phone,' he told her, 'and when he appeared, after hitching a lift in an executive jet, she was over the moon. Next step is to get her back home.'

'Knoll Barton?' she asked.

He looked surprised. 'Switzerland. That's her home now.' His expression changed. 'We all have to leave some time. Life goes on and we have to go with it to new places with fresh people. We can't cling to the past, can we?'

'I wouldn't know. It depends on the past.' Tricia felt tears forming and he saw the brightness of her sad heart. 'I've never had such a background, but if I had, I'd fight to keep it. You just don't know what it is that you possess, or you'd never treat it so lightly,' she said bitterly.

'Canada's a new world, and I like the people there,' he said mildly, but seemed to watch her reaction closely.

'Where's my cassoulet? Just in time, I see,' said Josie accusingly, with a glance at the half-empty plate that Matthew was attacking with relish. She helped herself and also gave Tricia more. 'This is good. Why don't you give up nursing and cook for dinner parties, Tricia? When I marry a millionaire will you be my housekeeper and cook sublime meals for me and my family?'

'Now there's an idea!' Matthew laughed. 'She can't do both, can she? Which is it to be? Nurse Metcalf or a cordon bleu cook?'

'I'm a nurse,' Tricia said firmly. 'Anyone can cook.'

'I wish you'd tell that to my sisters,' he grinned.

'They don't need to cook,' she replied. 'They all have such wonderful lives that they can employ people to do that.'

'My sister in Canada is struggling to learn and is doing quite well, according to her husband. He says his indigestion is getting better!'

'You'll see her soon and be able to judge for yourself,' Tricia said, lightly, and busily scraped the last of the food into one dish to be taken round for second helpings as everyone had been served.

'I'll see to that. Have some salad and take the weight off your feet,' Josie suggested. 'Save me some fruit cake,' she ordered, with a belligerent look at Matthew, who was dropping cake crumbs on to the table.

'Sit there,' Matthew insisted, and served a plate of salad with the last of the garlic bread. 'Cooks never have enough to eat.' He perched on the table beside her and finished his cake. 'You gave my notes?'

'Yes.' Tricia felt shy. 'Dr Jeffrey was a bit put out, but I didn't explain why you wouldn't be back at Beattie's.'

'So you aren't that close to him?' he queried.

'No.' She looked surprised. 'He invited me to dinner the night you gave us both a lift and I invited him to my party tonight.'

'Not exactly a cosy little tête-à-tête.'

'No.'

'I'm glad,' he said softly. 'Tricia, it was good to have you there when we found Maureen. I know you like her and she likes you, and yet you didn't fuss.'

'There wasn't time for hysterics, but I felt terrible afterwards in the train,' she confessed.

'Poor darling!' He took away her empty plate and held her hand, sending waves of bliss up through her entire body. 'I shall have to make it up to you, but now there's so much to do.' He stood up and kissed her gently. 'I have to phone the hospital and then do some paperwork about Canada.'

Tricia felt the glow die and braced herself to sound noncommittal. 'I see. Please don't let me keep you. I believe Sister King also has to settle her future in Canada. She's heard that she has the job she applied for.'

'Yes, I know. I saw her just now and she was full of her own good news.' Matthew looked at her apologetically. 'Everything changes, and I've decided to sell the cottages. Whatever I do, I shall have no need of them, and I can decide about Knoll Barton later. Can you give me the address of your parents?' he added. 'You said they wanted a base in the UK somewhere near a Naval centre. They're very good cottages,' he added. 'One is empty and one is rented out to a pleasant couple who might want to buy.'

'I don't know if they'd be what they want——' Tricia began.

'See for yourself,' he said, and produced a sheet of paper from his pocket with the address of a Devon estate agent on the heading. 'I'd like to think of people I know living there.'

'But you've never met them,' she protested.

'That could be remedied,' he said with a sweet smile, and left to find the phone.

'Not if you're in Canada,' she whispered sadly. 'Not if I never see you again.' She folded the paper to examine later, cut the cake into slices and took them in to the party.

CHAPTER NINE

'IT WAS a smashing party!' Dahlia Stephens swished water round the sink and dried the last of the instruments. 'A lot of work, but everyone was so happy.' She beamed and hummed a tune as she laid up the dressing trolley for Monsieur Bayard. 'Mr Masters is coming to see him, and you'd better be there to translate, Nurse Metcalf, but first do the water carafes and the in-take charts.'

'Yes, Nurse.' Tricia felt subdued. Everywhere she went she heard the same enthusiastic remarks about the party, and even those who hadn't been invited and turned up their noses at a first-year nurse having the cheek to take on such an undertaking were actually envious.

'Great party!' Josie said for the third time as they tidied beds. 'But what happened to lover-boy? I thought you'd invited him specially to repay him for taking you out to dinner.'

'I don't know. He disappeared after eating a huge helping of quiche and some salad and drinking most of the bottle of wine he brought!' Tricia tried to remember just when Paul had left, and thought it was after Matthew arrived.

'He doesn't get on with Dr Clancy,' Josie said. 'It's all the fault of Sister King, or so I heard. Paul Jeffrey used to date her fairly regularly, and then

our tawny-haired Romeo arrived and set every heart
aflutter—as *you* well know,' she added with a meaning look at Tricia.

'I don't know,' Tricia replied crossly. 'All I know
is that she's going to Canada and so is he, and he's
going to sell the wonderful house where he was
brought up. He's put the two cottages on the market,
and I suppose the rest will follow.'

'Uh-uh! Talk of the devil!' Josie groaned. 'I'll
finish the water jugs as Mr Masters has arrived in
the ward, making straight for Monsieur Bayard's
bed, and I think Paul Jeffrey is in the office with
Sister. Get the curtains round the bed quickly or
Sister will blow her top! Mr Masters thinks nothing
of stripping off the bedclothes for all the ward to
see. I wonder if he does that in women's wards?'

'Ah, Nurse.' Mr Masters looked pleased. 'Dressing trolley at once, and tell Nurse Stephens to come
here.' He smiled at the patient. 'Tell him I'm going
to take out the drain now.'

'I'd better tell Nurse Stephens you're ready, sir,'
Tricia said, and fled to the clinical-room, trying to
recall what drain was in French. She gasped, as Paul
Jeffrey came out of the office and they collided.

'Great party,' he said wryly. 'Or it could have
been if there'd been fewer people there. I hope you
realise that last night you changed my life, and I still
don't know if I want to change?'

'Sorry,' she said hurriedly. 'What's the French for
drain? Mr Masters is here. I have to fetch Nurse
Stephens.'

'Don't panic!' he laughed. 'No, I don't think it

would have worked out, but if it means anything to you, I was very tempted.' He bent to kiss her cheek. 'You're the sweetest, most aggravating female I've met, bar one.'

'Mr Masters?' Tricia repeated in alarm as she saw his head poking out between the curtains and he looked annoyed.

'OK, I'll sort it out,' Paul replied easily. He seemed very relaxed and not at all cross that his plans for last night had been foiled. 'You still owe me, but that can come later.' He walked away quickly and Tricia asked Dahlia to take in the trolley, mentioning that the surgeon wanted the drain taken out.

'Monsieur Bayard must be as tough as old boots,' Dahlia said, cheerfully. 'He had a bad infection and a lot of discharge to drain off from the pouch of Douglas as well as adhesions that had stuck down after several milder attacks he'd had at sea.' She pushed the trolley towards the bed. 'I'm glad he loses the drain today, as it was becoming very soggy round the stitches and that might have caused another problem. Bring me the pair of tiny narrow scissors in the sterilising solution. I may need them as the stitches will be embedded. Neither of us is going to enjoy this!'

Tricia rinsed the scissors in sterile water, holding them in long-handled Cheatles forceps and then putting them in a sterile kidney dish. She parted the curtains slightly, enough to put the dish down on the trolley, and backed away, but stopped to listen beyond the now closed curtains when she heard what Mr Masters was saying.

'What's wrong with England?' he asked. 'All I hear is Canada these days. It's bad enough losing a very efficient casualty sister, but we can ill afford to lose good doctors. As soon as I get used to them, they want a change. Is it me?' he added with a chuckle. 'I know I make life hell at times, but surely Canada is a bit far away to go to escape me?'

'Whoever works here at Beattie's takes away a lot of very good traditions and a lot of good ideas,' said Paul Jeffrey. 'It may be a wrench, but I know Sister King is looking forward to leaving.'

Tricia walked away slowly. By now Sister Ruth King must have told everyone of her plans, and surely had not omitted to mention the fact that Dr Clancy was leaving too. She went down for her coffee break and answered automatically, with a forced smile, as several people said how much they had enjoyed the party. 'Everyone was very helpful,' she said. 'I had no clearing up to do, as we threw away the plates and cups and forks and you greedy lot ate every scrap of food. Someone even washed the pots and pans while I was checking to see that there were no bits of rubbish on the floor and no cigarette ends in the flowerpots.' She smiled, warming to the friendliness that the party had generated. 'I did enjoy the cooking,' she admitted, 'so please don't think it was any trouble. It gave me a good excuse to indulge myself in my favourite hobby!'

After duty, she finished the letter she had begun to her parents and looked again at the description of the cottage on the estate of Knoll Barton. If they bought it, she dreamed to herself, she could at least visit the place where Matthew had once lived, and she had to admit that the cottage was just what her parents would love to own, after years of married quarters and faceless hotels and rented apartments. It wouldn't be fair to deprive them of the chance to buy such a place, she decided, and folded it to fit the envelope with her letter.

Once it was posted, she regretted it, but it was now too late to change her mind. Matthew would be gone soon and her work would take all her energies and thoughts. She rang the cottage hospital, only to be told that Maureen had been flown out by private ambulance plane to Geneva. The ward sister recognised her voice and added, 'Her fiancé came and made the arrangements, and they're to be married as soon as she's really fit. Isn't it romantic? He's very wealthy and obviously adores her.'

Maureen to be married, and Ruth King would get her man too, once she turned his head firmly towards Canada. Joy for some, but Tricia lay across her bed, with tears in her eyes, remembering every word that Matthew had said to her, every smile, and every touch that had sent such waves of desire through her, body and soul.

She went to the shower-room to freshen up before supper and to make sure there were no signs of tears. A faint smile surfaced as she remembered the night when Matthew caught her half naked as she dashed to her room for her shower cap. This time she zipped up her robe firmly and carried the terrible cap with her toilet bag, and of course met nobody, but as she emerged, relaxed and fragrant, the urgency of the telephone made her run down, still in her bathrobe, to answer it.

'Nurses' hostel, the Princess Beatrice,' she said.

'Tricia?' She started at the sound of the deep voice, warm and pleased to hear her.

'Where are you?' she asked. It was an outside line, from a callbox.

'Half an hour outside London, but I wanted to catch you before you went out for the evening,' said Matthew.

'Not tonight. Just salad in the cafeteria, as there was nothing left after last night,' she said, and laughed.

'Wait for me. I'm hungry, and we'll have something in the Falcon. Maureen wants to give you a present, and if I don't deliver it I may put it down and lose it,' he added cheerfully, 'so you'd better be there.' He rang off, and Tricia went slowly up to her room.

Matthew had sounded in a very good mood. He had every right to be so, with his sister recovered from the accident and going to marry a wealthy man. There were other reasons too, she thought. One wedding often triggered off another, and the fact that he faced a whole new life was exciting.

So I have to watch him eat dinner, and want him with every fibre of my being while he tells me his plans. I may hear of Maureen's wedding plans too, but his inmost thoughts will be far away across the ocean where I shall never go. This might be the last time I have dinner with him, she thought with a sense of loss. No Maureen to visit, and Sister Ruth would make sure he didn't stray far now until she really had him tied to her side.

Almost defiantly, she opened her cupboard door and took out a shirt of muted flame-coloured silk, heavily embroidered with flowers and Eastern designs, that hung gently on her shoulders and softly over her breasts. It was a gift from her parents and said to be part of the gifts a bride would have at her wedding, in the Far East. The tightly fitting black silk trousers that went with it hugged her slender hips and made her look taller and very supple as the silk glinted in the light. Plain black shiny pumps and a purse studded with fake jewels, from Singapore, transformed her into something far more exotic than she had ever dared to be, and she caught her breath. For a moment she hesitated, ready to tear off the clothes and dress in plain jeans and shirt, but she stopped.

Why not show him just once that she could be glamorous, and maybe once in a while, when he was away from England and had lost Knoll Barton, he might remember the girl who had annoyed him, intrigued him, fed him and, if he could still admit it, had attracted him?

The light woollen throw seemed the most realistic thing to wear as her jackets of denim and cord looked odd with the silk, and the colours were rich and picked out the flame and peacock green of the embroidery. Matthew called up the stairs, 'Tricia?' and she walked slowly down to meet him. He stared, and she felt the hair at the back of her neck rise. Well, he really had noticed, even with the wide shawl covering most of the shirt.

'I'm ready,' she said. 'Where's my pressie?' She felt a bright thread of awareness forming between them and tried to sound light.

'Oh, damn, I left it in the car.' Matthew seemed about to touch her, then turned away. 'You shall have it once I'm fed,' he said firmly, and climbed into the driver's seat, leaving her to open her own door, and the gears crashed as he backed to go down the drive. 'Sorry,' he muttered. 'I seem to have been driving all day.' He took a deep breath and drove slowly. 'Maureen sends her love,' he said at last. 'I went to the airport to see them off at a small airfield in Devon where a lot of private planes take off for domestic flights, but of course, Karl got clearance to fly to Geneva from there.'

'Of course,' Tricia agreed. Wealth and influence could move mountains, but she had no such influence to keep the one man she would ever really love by her side.

'Your hair's wet,' she said.

'Drying fast,' he assured her. 'But I was hot and dusty and needed a shower.' He grinned. 'No nice bath cap to keep me dry.'

'I'm more careful when going along the corridor now,' Tricia said demurely.

'I went back to the manor to pack everything Maureen had left there, as she now feels free of the place for ever. Karl will fill her life, and her work will take a lot of time.'

'She made the house look beautiful,' Tricia said, remembering her bedroom there and the delicate shades of eau-de-Nil and pale pink of the small drawing-room, and the rustic charm of the kitchen.

'That helped her to tear herself away from our family past. It became a job of work just as many others she does each year, and once it was finished, she was free.' Matthew slid the shawl from her shoulders as they entered the Falcon and traced the pattern of a flower on the sleeve of the shirt. 'Beautiful,' he said softly, and his voice held a caress. 'Come on, I'm starving!' He strode into the restaurant, and she followed.

'Did she change every room?' she asked.

'Only the ground floor and the main bedrooms, but Maureen never went into the other rooms. She said they were too tatty and the wrong shape for her plans, but I think she hated to see the old nursery and the room where my mother sewed and made a mess with cotton threads and silk embroidery.' He looked pensive. 'I found a few things we hadn't seen for years and a lot of old jewellery. Maureen took a brooch and some pearls that she had as a child, but she wants me to get rid of the rest. The others took all their belongings when they left home, so I'm free to sell it or give it away.'

He picked up the menu and they chose their food while the waiter hovered and conversation was difficult, but as soon as the order was taken, Tricia said, 'How can you bear to sell what must have been precious to your mother?'

'I can give it away if that's more acceptable to

you,' Matthew said, and smiled, his glance lingering on the soft curves hinted at through the thin silk. 'Do you like amber? Real amber that's warm to the touch? It would go with that very well.'

'I daresay, but surely you want to keep some in the family?'

'Some,' he agreed. He raised a hand to wave to a couple who sat at the other end of the restaurant, and Tricia blinked. It was a mirror image of the last time she was in the Falcon when she had been with Paul and Matthew had been with Ruth King, the couples sitting at these same tables, but now she was with Matthew and Paul was obviously very engrossed with the sister from Casualty.

Ruth King regarded Tricia with interest but no animosity, taking in the pretty shirt and her general appearance but pleased with her own dress of dark blue chiffon.

'Yes, they've made it up,' said Matthew. 'I think he drank too much last night and lost his head. I hear he told Ruth that if she went to Canada then he ought to go too, to spare her from the embarrassment of not speaking French, as her hospital is close to Quebec and many of the patients prefer French.'

'What a lovely party you'll be. Three from Beattie's is quite a lot,' Tricia remarked, suddenly finding that her appetite had gone.

'Three? I'm not going with them to Quebec,' said Matthew.

'You'll be in Canada,' she replied as if the country was as small as the Isle of Man.

He laughed. 'I may go later for six months or a

year, but I've decided to stay in England and take a half-share in a private hospital in Devon. That's why I need capital from the sale of the cottages and a bit of land that doesn't matter as far as views from the manor are affected, but will be valuable to a developer.'

'You'll keep Knoll Barton?' Her eyes misted with tears. 'I'm glad,' she said simply, then remembered that she'd sent details of the cottage to her parents. It would be worse; having him at the manor when she was visiting her parents would only make her heartache more acute.

'Eat up,' ordered Matthew. 'I hate to see a girl pick at her food. I know it isn't a patch on what you can make, but they do their best.'

'It's delicious,' she said, and obediently ate her halibut and broccoli. He isn't leaving England! she thought. He'll be at Beattie's for ages yet and then at Knoll Barton, and even if I can't have him as my own, I can see him, speak to him, and maybe in time he might want to make love to me.

'You haven't seen your present yet,' he reminded her when they reached the hostel. 'Coffee in your room?'

She nodded, wondering why silk gave an added frisson of sexuality to each time they touched. She filled the coffee filter and was glad her room was tidy. She bit her lip. One of us will have to sit on the bed, she thought. Junior nurses had only one chair. Matthew watched her as she busied herself with pretty coffee mugs and opened the now almost empty biscuit tin. Her face held a sweet unease that made his eyes tender. 'All the shadows of your changing face,' he murmured, half recalling a poem and knowing now what it meant, but she didn't seem to hear. He opened the wooden box that had seen many better days and needed a new clasp. He tipped the contents on the bed and stirred them with one finger.

'Aladdin's cave,' said Tricia, and held up a jewelled butterfly that had a comb attached.

'Here. Maureen said they'd suit you, and she was right.' He slid the long string of heavy amber beads over her head and they sat on the silk shirt and channelled a cleft between her breasts. Tricia sighed as he kissed her cheeks, then her fluttering eyelids, and his hands caressed the beads and the soft flesh through the silk. His mouth was urgent, as if he had longed for her kisses with a hunger that was impossible to satisfy, and she clung to him as if in fear of shipwreck and being cast up on a cold and lonely shore. At last he moved away and laughed shakily. 'Damn pin!' he said, and found that he'd sat on a gold and opal brooch. Tricia watched him and wanted the dream to go on for ever, for it must be a dream.

'Now, we have to be sensible,' he said. 'Don't look at me like that, woman!' He kissed her again. 'Now behave! I suppose you want to be a nurse? Have a department and boss every man in sight?'

'I enjoy nursing,' she replied.

'After two years, could you bear to leave without being registered?'

'Are you offering me a job, sir?' She caught her breath.

'I might,' Matthew replied. 'It carries certain conditions.' He took a small box from the mass of gold and silver and trinkets and opened it. 'I'm a lazy so-and-so in some things, and this was going spare.' He rubbed the ring on the sleeve of his jacket and the rubies glowed as brightly as they had done a hundred years ago. He took Tricia's left hand and slowly placed the ring on her finger. 'That's one of the conditions: that you wear my grandmother's ring and say you love me.' He kissed her gently. 'Could you give up all this?' He eyed the rather plain room with amusement. 'Could you bear to change it for Knoll Barton?'

'I will,' she said.

'Saying that comes much later; say next month?' he said. 'This time I'll buy a ring, or two rings for us to exchange if you want to tie me for life.'

'Two rings,' she agreed. 'Can you give up Canada? Really without caring?'

Matthew laughed. 'As soon as I knew Ruth had applied to go there, I backed out and suggested Jeffrey as a substitute. He's a good doctor, and they're made for each other.'

'As we are?' Shyly, Tricia let him unbutton the shirt and let it slip from her body. His hands were all she desired, his mouth wandering over the soft skin a delirium of ecstasy, and his body perfect in homage and desire.

present
Sally Wentworth's 50th Romance
The Golden Greek

Sally Wentworth has been writing for Mills & Boon for nearly 14 years. Her books are sold worldwide and translated into many different languages.

The Golden Greek, her 50th best selling romance will be available in the shops from December 1991, priced at £1.60.

— MEDICAL ROMANCE —

The books for your enjoyment this month are:

MEDICAL DECISIONS Lisa Cooper
DEADLINE LOVE Judith Worthy
NO TIME FOR ROMANCE Kathleen Farrell
RELATIVE ETHICS Caroline Anderson

♥ ♥ ♥ ♥ ♥

Treats in store!

Watch next month for the following absorbing stories:

ALL FOR LOVE Margaret Barker
HOMETOWN HOSPITAL Lydia Balmain
LOVE CHANGES EVERYTHING Laura MacDonald
A QUESTION OF HONOUR Margaret O'Neill

Available from Boots, Martins, John Menzies, W.H. Smith and other paperback stockists.

Also available from Mills and Boon Reader Service, P.O. Box 236, Thornton Road, Croydon, Surrey CR9 3RU.

Readers in South Africa — write to:
Independent Book Services Pty, Postbag X3010, Randburg, 2125, S. Africa.